Black Spirits & White

Cram Ralph Adams

Contents

BLACK SPIRITS & WHITE

BY

Cram, Ralph Adams

No. 252 Rue M. le Prince.

WHEN in May, 1886, I found myself at last in Paris, I naturally determined to throw myself on the charity of an old chum of mine, Eugene Marie d'Ardeche, who had forsaken Boston a year or more ago on receiving word of the death of an aunt who had left him such property as she possessed. I fancy this windfall surprised him not a little, for the relations between the aunt and nephew had never been cordial, judging from Eugene's remarks touching the lady, who was, it seems, a more or less wicked and witch-like old person, with a penchant for black magic, at least such was the common report.

Why she should leave all her property to d'Ardeche, no one could tell, unless it was that she felt his rather hobbledehoy tendencies towards Buddhism and occultism might some day lead him to her own unhallowed height of questionable illumination. To be sure d'Ardeche reviled her as a bad old woman, being himself in that state of enthusiastic exaltation which sometimes accompanies a boyish fancy for occultism; but in spite of his distant and repellent attitude, Mlle. Blaye de Tartas made him her sole heir, to the violent wrath of a questionable old party known to infamy as the Sar Torrevieja, the "King of the Sorcerers." This malevolent old portent, whose gray and crafty face was often seen in the Rue M. le Prince during the life of Mlle, de Tartas had, it seems, fully expected to enjoy her small wealth after her death; and when it appeared that she had left him only the contents of the gloomy old house in the Quartier Latin, giving the house itself and all else of which she died possessed to her nephew in America, the Sar proceeded to remove everything from the place, and then to curse it elaborately and comprehensively, together with all those who should ever dwell therein.

Whereupon he disappeared.

This final episode was the last word I received from Eugene, but I knew the number of the house, 252 Rue M. le Prince. So, after a day or two given to a first cursory survey of Fans, I started across the Seine to find Eugene and compel him to do the honors of the city.

Every one who knows the Latin Quarter knows the Rue M. le Prince, running up the hill towards the Garden of the Luxembourg. It is full of queer houses and odd corners, — or was in '86, — and certainly No. 252 was, when I found it, quite as queer as any. It was nothing but a doorway, a black arch of old stone between and under two new houses painted yellow. The effect of this bit of seventeenth century masonry, with its dirty old doors, and rusty broken lantern sticking gaunt and grim out over the narrow sidewalk, was, in its frame of fresh plaster, sinister in the extreme.

I wondered if I had made a mistake in the number; it was quite evident that no one lived behind those cobwebs. I went into the doorway of one of the new hotels and interviewed the

No, M. d'Ardeche did not live there, though to be sure he owned the mansion; he himself resided in Meudon, in the country house of the late Mlle. de Tartas. Would Monsieur like the number and the street?

Monsieur would like them extremely, so I took the card that the concierge wrote for me, and forthwith started for the river, in order that I might take a steam-boat for Meudon. By one of those coincidences which happen so often, being quite inexplicable, I had not gone twenty paces down the street before I ran directly into the arms of Eugene d'Ardeche. In three minutes we were sitting in the queer little garden of the Chien Bleu, drinking vermouth and absinthe, and talking it all over.

You do not live in your aunt's house? I said at last interrogatively.

"No, but if this sort of thing keeps on I snail have to. I like Meudon much better, and the house is perfect, all furnished, and nothing in it newer than the last century. You must come out with me to-night and see it. I have got a jolly room fixed up for my Buddha. But there is something wrong with this house opposite. I can't keep a tenant in it, — not four days. I have had three, all within six months, but the stories have gone around and a man would as soon think of hiring the Cour des Comptes to live in as No. 252. It is notorious. The fact is, it is haunted the worst way.

I laughed and ordered more vermouth.

"That is all right. It is haunted all the same, or enough to keep it empty, and the funny part is that no one knows _how_ it is haunted. Nothing is ever seen, nothing heard. As far as I can find out, people just have the horrors and have them so bad they have to go to the hospital afterwards. I have one extenant in the Bic6tre now. So the house stands empty, and as it covers considerable ground and is taxed for a lot, I don't know what to do about it. I think I'll either give it to that child of sin, Torrevieja, or else go and live in it myself. I shouldn't mind the ghosts, I am sure."

"Did you ever stay there ?"

"No, but I have always intended to, and in fact I came up here to-day to see a couple of rake-hell fellows I know, Fargeau and Duchesne, doctors in the Clinical Hospital beyond here, up by the Pare Mont Souris. They promised that they would spend the night with me some time in my aunt's house,—which is called around here, you must know, 'la Bouche d'Enfer,'—and I thought perhaps they would make it this week, if they can get off duty. Come up with me while I see them, and then we can go across the river to Véfour's and have some luncheon, you can get your things at the Chatham, and we will go out to Meudon, where of course you will spend the night with me.

The plan suited me perfectly, so we went up to the hospital, found Fargeau, who declared that he and Duchesne were ready for anything, the nearer the real bouche d' enfer" the better; that the following Thursday they would both be off duty for the night, and that on that day they would join in an attempt to outwit the devil and clear up the mystery of No. 252.

"Does M. l'Américain go with us ?" asked Fargeau.

"Why of course," I replied, "I intend to go, and you must not refuse me, d'Ardeche; I decline to be put off. Here is a chance for you to do the honors of your city in a manner which is faultless. Show me a real live ghost, and I will forgive Paris for having lost the Jardin Mabille."

So it was settled.

Later we went down to Meudon and ate dinner in the terrace room of the villa which was all that d'Ardeche had said, and more, so utterly was its atmosphere that of the seventeenth century. At dinner Eugene told me more about his late aunt, and the queer goings on in the old house.

Mlle. Blaye lived, it seems, all alone, except for one female servant of her own age; a severe, taciturn creature, with massive Breton features and a Breton tongue, whenever she vouchsafed to use it. No one ever was seen to enter the door of No. 252 except Jeanne the servant and the Sar
Torrevieja, the latter coming constantly from none knew whither, and always entering, _never leaving._ Indeed, the neighbors, who for eleven years had watched the old sorcerer sidle crab-wise up to the bell almost every day, declared vociferously that _never_ had he been seen to leave the house. Once, when they decided to keep absolute guard, the watcher, none other than Maître Garceau of the Chien Bleu, after keeping his eyes fixed on the door from ten o'clock one morning when the Sar arrived until four in the afternoon, during which time the door was un-opened (he knew this, for had he not gummed a ten-centime stamp over the joint and was not the stamp unbroken) nearly fell down when the sinister figure of Tor-revieja slid wickedly by him with a dry "Pardon, Monsieur! "and disappeared again through the black doorway.

This was curious, for No. 252 was entirely surrounded by houses, its only windows opening on a courtyard into which no eye could look from the hôtels of the Rue M. le Prince and the Rue de l'Ecole, and the mystery was one of the choice possessions of the Latin Quarter.

Once a year the austerity of the place was broken, and the denizens of the whole quarter stood open-mouthed watching many carriages drive up to No. 252, many of them private, not a few with crests on the door panels, from all of them descending veiled female figures and men with, coat collars turned up. Then followed curious sounds of music from within, and those whose houses joined the blank walls of No. 252 became for the moment popular, for by placing the ear against the wall strange music could distinctly be heard, and the sound of monotonous chanting voices now and then. By dawn the last guest would have departed, and for another year the hotel of Mlle. de Tartas was ominously silent.

Eugene declared that he believed it was a celebration of "Walpurgisnacht," and certainly appearances favored such a fancy.

"A queer thing about the whole affair is," he said, the fact that every one in the street swears that about a month ago, while I was out in Concarneau for a visit, the music and voices were heard again, just as when my revered aunt was in the flesh. The house was perfectly empty, as I tell you, so it is quite possible that the good people were enjoying an hallucination."

I must acknowledge that these stories did not reassure me; in fact, as Thursday came near, I began to regret a little my determination to spend the night in the house. I was too vain to back down, however, and the perfect coolness of the two doctors, who ran down Tuesday to Meudon to make a few arrangements, caused me to swear that I would die of fright before I would flinch. I suppose I believed more or less in ghosts, I am sure now that I am older I believe in them, there are in fact few things I can _not_ believe. Two or three inexplicable things had happened to me, and, although this was before my adventure with Rendel in Pæstum, I had a strong predisposition to belive some things that I could not explain, wherein I was out of sympathy with the age.

Well, to come to the memorable night of the twelfth of June, we had made our preparations, and after depositing a big bag inside the doors of No. 252, went across to the Chien Bleu, where Fargeau and Duchesne turned up promptly, and. we sat down to the best dinner Père Garceau could create.

I remember I hardly felt that the conversation was in good taste. It began with various stories of Indian fakirs and Oriental jugglery, matters in which Eugene was curiously well read, swerved to the horrors of the great Sepoy mutiny, and thus to reminiscences of the dissecting-room. By this time we had drunk more or less, and Duchesne launched into a photographic and Zolaesque account of the only time (as he said) when he was possessed of the panic of fear; namely, one night many years ago, when he was locked by accident into the dissecting-room of the Loucine, together with several cadavers of a rather unpleasant nature. I ventured to protest mildly against the choice of subjects, the result being a perfect carnival of horrors, so that when we finally drank our last _crème de cacao_ and started for "la Bouche d'Enfer," my nerves were in a somewhat rocky condition.

It was just ten o'clock when we came into the street. A hot dead wind drifted in great puffs through the city, and ragged masses of vapor swept the purple sky; an unsavory night altogether, one of those nights of hopeless lassitude when one feels, if one is at home, like doing nothing but drink mint juleps and smoke cigarettes.

Eugene opened the creaking door, and tried to light one of the lanterns; but the gusty wind blew out every match, and we finally had to close the outer doors before we could get a light. At last we had all the lanterns going, and I began to look around curiously. We were in a long, vaulted passage, partly carriageway, partly footpath, perfectly bare but for the street refuse which had drifted in with eddying winds. Beyond lay the courtyard, a curious place rendered more curious still by the fitful moonlight and the flashing of four dark lanterns. The place had evidently been once a most noble palace. Opposite rose the oldest portion, a three-story wall of the time of Francis I., with a great wisteria vine covering half. The wings on either side were more modern, seventeenth century, and ugly, while towards the street was nothing but a flat unbroken wall.

The great bare court, littered with bits of paper blown in by the wind, fragments of packing cases, and straw, mysterious with flashing lights and flaunting shadows, while low masses of torn vapor drifted overhead, hiding, then revealing the stars, and all in absolute silence, not even the sounds of the streets entering this prison-like place, was weird and uncanny in the extreme. I must confess that already I began to feel a slight disposition towards the horrors, but with that curious inconsequence which so often happens in the case of those who are deliberately growing scared, I could think of nothing more reassuring than those delicious verses of Lewis Carroll's: —

Just the place for a Snark! I have said it twice, That alone should encourage the crew.

Just the place for a Snark! I have said it thrice, What I tell you three times is true," —

which kept repeating themselves over and over in my brain with feverish insistence.

Even the medical students had stopped their chaffing, and were studying the surroundings gravely.

"There is one thing certain," said Fargeau, _"anything_ might have happened here without the slightest chance of discovery. Did ever you see such a perfect place for lawlessness ? "

"And _anything_ might happen here now, with the same certainty of impunity," continued Duchesne, lighting his pipe, the snap of the match making us all start. "D'Ardeche, your lamented relative was certainly well fixed; she had full scope here for her traditional experiments in demonology."

"Curse me if I don't believe that those same traditions were more or less founded on fact, said Eugene. I never saw this court under these conditions before, but I could believe anything now. What's that!

"Nothing but a door slamming." Said Duchesne, loudly.

"Well, I wish doors wouldn't slam in houses that have been empty eleven months.

"It is irritating," and Duchesne slipped his arm through mine; "but we must take things as they come. Remember we have to deal not only with the spectral lumber left here by your scarlet aunt, but as well with the supererogatory curse of that hell-cat Torrevieja. Come on! let's get inside before the hour arrives for the sheeted dead to squeak and gibber in these lonely halls. Light your pipes, your tobacco is a sure protection against ' your whoreson dead bodies'; light up and move on.

We opened the hall door and entered a vaulted stone vestibule, full of dust, and cobwebby.

"There is nothing on this floor," said Eugene, "except servants rooms and offices, and I don't believe there is anything wrong with them. I never heard that there was, any way. Let's go up stairs."

So far as we could see, the house was apparently perfectly uninteresting inside, all eighteenth century work, the façade of the main building being, with the vestibule, the only portion of the Francis I. work.

"The place was burned during the Terror," said Eugene, "for my great-uncle, from whom Mlle, de Tartas inherited it, was a good and true Royalist; he went to Spain after the Revolution, and did not come back until the accession of Charles X., when he restored the house, and. then died, enormously old. This explains why it is all so new."

The old Spanish sorcerer to whom Mlle. de Tartas had left her personal property had done his work thoroughly. The house was absolutely empty, even the wardrobes and bookcases built in had been carried away; we went through room after room, finding all absolutely dismantled, only the windows and doors with their casings, the parquet floors, and the florid Renaissance mantels remaining.

"I feel better," remarked Fargeau. "The house may be haunted, but it don't look it, certainly; it is the most respectable place imaginable."

Just you wait," replied Eugene. "These are only the state apartments, which my aunt seldom used, except, perhaps, on her annual walpurgisnacht. Come up stairs and I will show you a better _mise en scène_."

On this floor, the rooms fronting the court, the sleeping-rooms, were quite small, — ("They are the bad rooms all the same," said Eugene,)—four of them, all just as ordinary in appearance as those below. A corridor ran behind them connecting with the wing corridor, and from this opened a door, unlike any of the other doors in that it was covered with green baize, somewhat moth-eaten. Eugene selected a key from the bunch he carried, unlocked the door, and with some difficulty forced it to swing inward; it was as heavy as the door of a safe.

"We are now, he said, "on the very threshold of hell itself; these rooms in here were my scarlet aunt's unholy of unholies. I never let them with the rest of the house, but keep them as a curiosity. I only wish Torrevieja had kept out; as it was, he looted them, as he did the rest of the house, and nothing is left but the walls and ceiling and floor. They are something, however, and may suggest what the former condition must have been. Tremble and The first apartment was a kind of anteroom, a cube of perhaps twenty feet each way, without windows, and with no doors except that by which we entered and another to the right. Walls, floor, and ceiling were covered with a black lacquer, brilliantly polished, that flashed the light of our lanterns in a thousand intricate reflections. It was like the inside of an enormous Japanese box, and about as empty. From this we passed to another room, and here we nearly dropped our lanterns. The room was circular, thirty feet or so in diameter, covered by a hemispherical dome; walls and ceiling were dark blue, spotted with gold stars; and reaching from floor to floor across the dome stretched a colossal figure in red lacquer of a nude woman kneeling, her legs reaching out along the floor on either side, her head touching the lintel of the door through which we had entered, her arms forming its sides, with the fore arms extended and stretching along the walls until they met the long feet. The most astounding, misshapen, absolutely terrifying thing, I think, I ever saw. From the navel hung a great white object, like the traditional roes egg of the Arabian Nights. The floor was of red lacquer, and in it was inlaid a pentagram the size of the room, made of wide strips of brass. In the centre of this pentagram was a circular disk of black stone, slightly saucer-shaped, with a small outlet in the middle.

The effect of the room was simply crushing, with this gigantic red figure crouched, over it all, the staring eyes fixed on one, no matter what his position. None of us spoke, so oppressive was the whole thing.

The third room was like the first in dimensions, but instead of being black it was entirely sheathed with plates of brass, walls, ceiling, and floor, — tarnished now, and turning green, but still brilliant under the lantern light. In the middle stood an oblong altar of porphyry, its longer dimensions on the axis of the suite of rooms, and at one end, opposite the range of doors, a pedestal of black basalt.

This was all. Three rooms, stranger than these, even in their emptiness, it would be hard to imagine. In Egypt, in India, they would not be entirely out of place, but here in Paris, in a commonplace _hôtel_, in the Rue M. le Prince, they were incredible.

We retraced our steps, Eugene closed the iron door with its baize covering, and we went into one of the front chambers and sat down, looking at each other.

"Nice party, your aunt," said Fargeau. "Nice old party, with amiable tastes; I am glad we are not to spend the night in _those_ rooms."

"What do you suppose she did there? inquired Duchesne. "I know more or less about black art, but that series of rooms is too much me.

"My impression is," said d'Ardeche, that the brazen room was a kind of sanctuary containing some image or other on the basalt base, while the stone in front was really an altar, — what the nature of the sacrifice might be I don't even guess. The round room may have been used for invocations and. incantations. The pentagram looks like it. Any way it is all just about as queer and _fin de siècle_ as I can well imagine. Look here, it is nearly twelve, let's dispose of ourselves, if we are going to hunt this thing down."

The four chambers on this floor of the old house were those said to be haunted, the wings being quite innocent, and, so far as we knew, the floors below. It was arranged that we should each occupy a room, leaving the doors open with the lights burning, and at the slightest cry or knock we were all to rush at once to the room from which the warning sound might come. There was no communication between the rooms to be sure, but, as the doors all opened into the corridor, every sound was plainly audible.

The last room fell to me, and I looked it over carefully.

It seemed innocent enough, a commonplace, square, rather lofty Parisian sleeping-room, finished in wood painted white, with a small marble mantel, a dusty floor of inlaid maple and cherry, walls hung with an ordinary French paper, apparently quite new, and two deeply embrasured windows looking out on the court.

I opened the swinging sash with some trouble, and sat down in the window seat with my lantern beside me trained on the only door, which gave on the corridor.

The wind had gone down, and it was very still without, — still and hot. The masses of luminous vapor were gathering thickly overhead, no longer urged by the gusty wind. The great masses of rank wisteria leaves, with here and there a second blossoming of purple flowers, hung dead over the window in the sluggish air. Across the roofs I could hear the sound of a belated _fiacre_ in the streets below. I filled my pipe again and waited.

For a time the voices of the men in the other rooms were a companionship, and at first I shouted to them now and then, but my voice echoed rather unpleasantly through the long corridors, and had a suggestive way of reverberating around the left wing beside me, and coming out at a broken window at its extremity like the voice of another man. I soon gave up my attempts at conversation, and devoted myself to the task of keeping awake.

It was not easy; why did I eat that lettuce salad at Père Garceau's? I should have known better. It was making me irresistibly sleepy, and wakefulness was absolutely necessary. It was certainly gratifying to know that I could sleep, that my courage was by me to that extent, but in the interests of science I must keep awake. But almost never, it seemed, had sleep looked so desirable. Half a hundred times, nearly, I would doze for an instant, only to awake with a start, and find my pipe gone out. Nor did the exertion of relighting it pull me together. I struck my match mechanically, and with the first puff dropped off again. It was most vexing. I got up and walked around the room. It was most annoying. My cramped position had almost put both my legs to sleep. I could hardly stand. I felt numb, as though with cold. There was no longer any sound from the other rooms, nor from without. I sank down in my window seat. How dark it was growing ! I turned up the lantern. That Pipe again, how obstinately it kept going out! and my last match was gone. The lantern, too, was _that_ going out? I lifted my hand to turn it up again. It felt like lead, and fell beside me.

Then I awoke, — absolutely. I remembered the story of "The Haunters and the Haunted. _This_ was the Horror. I tried to rise, to cry out. My body was like lead, my tongue was paralyzed. I could hardly move my eyes. And the light was going out. There was no question about that. Darker and darker yet; little by little the pattern of the paper was swallowed up in the advancing night. A prickling numbness garnered in every nerve, my right arm slipped without feeling from my lap to my side, and I could not raise it, — it swung helpless. A thin, keen humming began in my head, like the cicadas on a hillside in September. The darkness was coming fast.

Yes, this was it. Something was subjecting me, body and mind, to slow paralysis. Physically I was already dead. If I could only hold my mind, my consciousness, I might still be safe, but could I? Could I resist the mad horror of this silence, the deepening dark, the creeping numbness? I knew that, like the man in the ghost story, my only safety lay here.

It had come at last. My body was dead, I could no longer move my eyes. They were fixed in that last look on the place where the door had been, now only a deepening of the dark.

Utter night: the last flicker of the lantern was gone. I sat and waited; my mind was still keen, but how long would it last ? There was a limit even to the endurance of the utter panic of fear.

Then the end began. In the velvet blackness came two white eyes, milky, opalescent, small, faraway, —awful eyes, like a dead dream. More beautiful than I can describe, the flakes of white flame moving from the perimeter inward, disappearing in the centre, like a never ending flow of opal water into a circular tunnel. I could not have moved my eyes had I possessed the power: they devoured the fearful, beautiful things that grew slowly, slowly larger, fixed on me, advancing, growing more beaufiful, the white flakes of light sweeping more swiftly into the blazing vortices, the awful fascination deepening in its insane intensity as the white, vibrating eyes grew nearer, larger.

Like a hideous and implacable engine of death the eyes of the unknown Horror swelled and expanded until they were close before me, enormous, terrible, and I felt a slow, cold, wet breath propelled with mechanical regularity against my face, enveloping me in its fetid mist, in its charnel-house deadliness.

With ordinary fear goes always a physical but with me in the presence of this unspeakable Thing was only the utter and awful terror of the mind, the mad fear of a prolonged and ghostly nightmare. Again and again I tried to shriek, to make some noise, but physically I was utterly dead. I could only feel myself go mad with the terror of hideous death. The eyes were close on me, — their movement so swift that they seemed to be but palpitating names, the dead breath was around me like the depths of the deepest sea.

Suddenly a wet. icy mouth, like that of a dead cuttle-fish, shapeless, jelly-like, fell over mine. The horror began slowly to draw my life from me, but, as enormous and shuddering folds of palpitating jelly swept sinuously around me, my will came back, my body awoke with the reaction of final fear, and I closed with the nameless death that enfolded me.

What was it that I was fighting ? My arms sunk through the unresisting mass that was turning me to ice. Moment by moment new folds of cold jelly swept round me, crushing me with the force of Titans. I fought to wrest my mouth from this aw-ful Thing that sealed it, but, if ever I succeeded and caught a single breath, the wet, sucking mass closed over my face again before I could cry out. I think I fought for hours, desperately, insanely, in a silence that was more hideous than any sound, — fought until I felt final death at hand, until the memory of all my life rushed over me like a flood, until I no longer had strength to wrench my face from that hellish succubus, until with a last mechanical struggle I fell and yielded to death.

Then I heard a voice say, "If he is dead, I can never forgive myself; I was to blame."

Another replied, "He is not dead, I know we can save him if only we reach the hospital in time. Drive like hell, _cocker_! twenty francs for you, if you get there in three minutes.

Then there was night again, and nothingness, until I suddenly awoke and stared around. I lay in a hospital ward, very white and sunny, some yellow _fleurs-de-lis_ stood beside the head of the pallet, and a tall sister of mercy sat by my side.

To tell the story in a few words, I was in the Hôtel Dieu, where the men had taken me that fearful night of the twelfth of June. I asked for Fargeau or Duchesne, and by and by the latter came, and sitting beside the bed told me all that I did not know.

It seems that they had sat, each in his room, hour after hour, hearing nothing, very much bored, and disappointed. Soon after two o'clock Fargeau, who was in the next room, called to me to ask if I was awake. I gave no reply, and, after shouting once or twice, he took his lantern and came to investigate. The door was locked on the inside ! He instantly called d'Ardeche and Duchesne, and together they hurled themselves against the door. It resisted. Within they could hear irregular footsteps dashing here and there, with heavy breathing. Although frozen with terror, they fought to destroy the door and finally succeeded by using a great slab of marble that formed the shelf of the mantel in Fargeau's room. As the door crashed in, they were suddenly hurled back against the walls of the corridor, as though by an explosion, the lanterns were extinguished, and they found themselves in utter silence and darkness.

As soon as they recovered from the shock, they leaped into the room and fell over my body in the middle of the floor. They lighted one of the lanterns, and saw the strangest sight that can be imagined. The floor and walls to the height of about six feet were running with something that seemed like stagnant water, thick, glutinous, sickening. As for me, I was drenched with the same cursed liquid. The odor of musk was nauseating. They dragged me away, stripped off my clothing, wrapped me in their coats, and hurried to the hospital, thinking me perhaps dead. Soon after sunrise d'Ardeche left the hospital, being assured that I was in a fair way to recovery, with time, and with Fargeau went up to examine by daylight the traces of the adventure that was so nearly fatal. They were too late. Fire engines were coming down the street as they passed the Academie. A neighbor rushed up to d'Ardeche:

"O Monsieur! what misfortune, yet what fortune! It is true _la Bouche d'Enfer_ — I beg pardon, the residence of the lamented Mlle. de Tartas, — was burned, but not wholly, only the ancient building. The wings were saved, and for that great credit is due the brave firemen. Monsieur will remember them, no doubt.

It was quite true. Whether a forgotten lantern, overturned in the excitement, had done the work, or whether the origin of the fire was more supernatural, it was certain that the Mouth of Hell was no more. A last engine was pumping slowly as d'Ardeche came up; half a dozen limp, and one distended, hose stretched through the _porte cockère_, and within only the facade of Francis I. remained, draped still with the black stems of the wisteria. Beyond lay a great vacancy, where thin smoke was rising slowly. Every floor was gone, and the strange halls of Mlle. Blaye de Tartas were only a memory.

With d'Ardeche I visited the place last year, but in the stead of the ancient walls was then only a new and ordinary building, fresh and respectable; yet the wonderful stories of the old _Bouche d'Enfer_ still lingered in the quarter, and will hold there, I do not doubt, until the Day of Judgment.

IN KROPFSBERG KEEP.

To the traveller from Innsbruck to Munich, up the lovely valley of the silver Inn, many castles appear, one after another, each on its beetling cliff or gentle hill, — appear and disappear, melting into the dark fir trees that grow so thickly on every side, — Laneck, Lichtwer, Ratholtz, Tratzberg, Matzen, Kropfsberg, gathering close around the entrance to the dark and wonderful Zillerthal.

But to us — Torn Rendel and myself — there are two castles only: not the gorgeous and princely Ambras, nor the noble old Tratzberg, with its crowded treasures of solemn and splendid mediaevalism; but little Matzen, where eager hospitality forms the new life of a never-dead chivalry, and Kropfsberg, ruined, tottering, blasted by fire and smitten with grievous years, —a dead thing, and haunted, — full of strange legends, and eloquent of mystery and tragedy.

We were visiting the von C —— s at Matzen, and gaming our first wondering knowledge of the courtly, cordial castle life in the Tyrol,— of the gentle and delicate hospitality of noble Austnans. Brixleg had ceased to be but a mark on a map, and had become a place of rest and delight, a home for homeless wanderers on the face of Europe, while Schloss Matzen was a synonym for all that was gracious and kindly and beautiful in life. The days moved on in a golden round of riding and driving and shooting: down to Landl and Thiersee for chamois, across the river to the magic Achensee, up the Zillerthal, across the Schmerner Joch, even to the railway station at Steinach. And in the evenings after the late dinners in the upper hall where the sleepy hounds leaned against our chairs looking at us with suppliant eyes, in the evenings when the fire was dying away in the hooded fireplace in the library, stories. Stories, and legends, and fairy tales, while the stiff old portraits changed countenance constantly under the flickering firelight, and the sound of the drifting Inn came softly across the meadows far below.

If ever I tell the Story of Schloss Matzen, then will be the time to paint the too inadequate picture of this fair oasis in the desert of travel and tourists and hotels; but just now it is Kropfsberg the Silent that is of greater importance, for it was only in Matzen that the story was told by Fräulein E——, the gold-haired niece of Frau von C——, one hot evening in July, when we were sitting in the great west window of the drawing-room after a long ride up the Stallenthal. All the windows were open to catch the faint wind, and we had sat for a long time watching the Otzethaler Alps turn rose-color over distant Innsbruck, then deepen to violet as the sun went down and the white mists rose slowly until Lichtwer and Laneck and Kropfsberg rose like craggy islands in a silver sea.

And this is the story as Fräulein E—— told it to us, the Story of Kropfsberg Keep.

A great many years ago, soon after my grandfather died, and Matzen came to us, when I was a little girl, and so young that I remember nothing of the affair except as something dreadful that frightened me very much, two young men who had studied painting with my grandfather came down to Brixleg from Munich, partly to paint, and partly to amuse themselves, ghost-hunting as they said, for they were very sensible young men and prided themselves on it, laughing at all kinds of "superstition," and particularly at that form which believed in ghosts and feared them. They had never seen a real ghost, you know, and they belonged to a certain set of people who believed nothing they had not seen themselves, — which always seemed to me _very_ conceited. Well, they knew that we had lots of beautiful castles here in the lower valley," and they assumed, and rightly, that every castle has at least _one_ ghost story connected with it, so they chose this as their hunting ground, only the game they sought was ghosts, not chamois. Their plan was to visit every place that was supposed to be haunted, and to meet every reputed ghost, and prove that it really was no ghost at all.

There was a little inn down in the village then, kept by an old man named Peter Rosskopf, and the two young men made this their headquarters. The very first night they began to draw from the old innkeeper all that he knew of legends and ghost stories connected with Brixleg and its castles, and as he was a most garrulous old gentleman he filled them with the wildest delight by his stones of the ghosts of the castles about the mouth of the Zillerthal. Of course the old man believed every word he said, and you can imagine his horror and amazement when, after story of Kropfsberg and its haunted keep, the elder of the two boys, whose surname I have forgotten, but whose Christian name was Rupert, calmly said, "Your story is most satisfactory: we will sleep in Kropfsberg Keep tomorrow night, and you must provide us with all that we may need to make ourselves comfortable.

The old man nearly fell into the fire. "What for a blockhead are you?" he cried, with big eyes. "The 'keep is haunted by Count Albert's ghost, I tell you!

"That is why we are going there tomorrow night; we wish to make the acquaintance of Count Albert." "But there was a man stayed there once, and in the morning he was dead.

"Very silly of him; there are two of us, and we carry revolvers.

"But it's a _ghost_, I tell you, almost screamed the innkeeper; "are ghosts afraid of firearms ?

"Whether they are or not, we are _not_ afraid of _them_?

Here the younger boy broke in, — he was named Otto von Kleist. I remember the name, for I had a music teacher once by that name. He abused the poor old man shamefully; told him that they were going to spend the night in Kropfsberg in spite of Count Albert and Peter Rosskopf, and that he might as well make the most of it and earn his money with cheerfulness.

In a word, they finally bullied the old fellow into submission, and when the morning came he set about preparing for the suicide, as he considered it, with sighs and mutterings and ominous shakings of the head.

You know the condition of the castle now,— nothing but scorched walls and crumbling piles of fallen masonry. Well, at the time I tell you of, the keep was still partially preserved. It was finally burned out only a few years ago by some wicked boys who came over from Jenbach to have a good time. But when the ghost hunters came, though the two lower floors had fallen into the crypt, the third floor remained. The peasants said it _could_ not fall, but that it would stay until the Day of Judgment, because it was in the room above that the wicked Count Albert sat watching the flames destroy the great castle and his imprisoned guests, and where he finally hung himself in a suit of armor that had belonged to his mediaeval ancestor, the first Count Kropfsberg.

No one dared touch him, and so he hung there for twelve years, and all the time venturesome boys and daring men used to creep up the turret steps and stare awfully through the chinks in the door at that ghostly mass of steel that held within itself the body of a murderer and suicide, slowly returning to the dust from which it was made. Finally it disappeared, none knew whither, and for another dozen years the room stood empty but for the old furniture and the rotting hangings.

So, when the two men climbed the stairway to the haunted room, they found a very different state of things from what exists now. The room was absolutely as it was left the night Count Albert burned the castle, except that all trace of the suspended suit of armor and its ghastly contents had vanished.

No one had dared to cross the threshold, and I suppose that for forty years no living thing had entered that dreadful room.

On one side stood a vast canopied bed of black wood, the damask hangings of which were covered with mould and mildew. All the clothing of the bed was in perfect order, and on it lay a book, open, and face downward. The only other furniture in the room consisted of several old chairs, a carved oak chest, and a big inlaid table covered with books and papers, and on one corner two or three bottles with dark solid sediment at the bottom, and a glass, also dark with the dregs of wine that had been poured out almost half a century before. The tapestry on the walls was green with mould, but hardly torn or otherwise defaced, for although the heavy dust of forty years lay on everything the room had been preserved from further harm. No spider web was to be seen, no trace of nibbling mice, not even a dead moth or fly on the sills of the diamond-paned windows; life seemed to have shunned the room utterly and finally.

The men looked at the room curiously, and, I am sure, not without some feelings of awe and unacknowledged fear; but, whatever they may have felt of instinctive shrinking, they said nothing, and quickly set to work to make the room passably inhabitable. They decided to touch nothing that had not absolutely to be changed, and therefore they made for themselves a bed in one corner with the mattress and linen from the inn. In the great fireplace they piled a lot of wood on the caked ashes of a fire dead for forty years, turned the old chest into a table, and laid out on it all their arrangements for the evening's amusement: food, two or three bottles of wine, pipes and tobacco, and the chess-board that was their inseparable travelling companion.

All this they did themselves: the innkeeper would not even come within the walls of the outer court; he insisted that he had washed his hands of the whole affair, the silly dunderheads might go to their death their own way. _He_ would not aid and abet them. One of the stable boys brought the basket of food and the wood and the bed up the winding stone stairs, to be sure, but neither money nor prayers nor threats would bring him within the walls of the accursed place, and he stared fearfully at the hare-brained boys as they worked around the dead old room preparing for the night that was coming so fast.

At length everything was in readiness, and after a final visit to the inn for dinner Rupert and Otto started at sunset for the Keep. Half the village went with them, for Peter Rosskopf had babbled the whole story to an open-mouthed crowd of wondering men and women, and as to an execution the awe-struck crowd followed the two boys dumbly, curious to see if they surely would put their plan into execution. But none went farther than the outer doorway of the stairs, for it was already growing twilight. In absolute silence they watched the two foolhardy youths with their lives in their hands enter the terrible Keep, standing like a tower in the midst of the piles of stones that had once formed walls joining it with the mass of the castle beyond. When a moment later a light showed itself in the high windows above, they sighed resignedly and went their ways, to wait stolidly until morning should come and prove the truth of their fears and warnings.

In the mean time the ghost hunters built a huge fire, lighted their many candles, and sat down to await developments. Rupert afterwards told my uncle that they really felt no fear whatever, only a contemptuous curiosity, and they ate their supper with good appetite and an unusual relish. It was a long evening. They played many games of chess, waiting for midnight. Hour passed after hour, and nothing occurred to interrupt the monotony of the evening. Ten, eleven, came and went,—it was almost midnight. They piled more wood in the fireplace, lighted new candles, looked to their pistols — and waited. The clocks in the village struck twelve; the sound coming muffled through the high, deepembrasured windows. Nothing happened, nothing to break the heavy silence; and with a feeling of disappointed relief they looked at each other and acknowledged that they had met another rebuff.

Finally they decided that there was no use in sitting up and boring themselves any longer, they had much better rest; so Otto threw himself down on the mattress, falling almost immediately asleep. Rupert sat a little longer, smoking, and watching the stars creep along behind the shattered glass and the bent leads of the lofty windows; watching the fire fall together, and the strange shadows move mysteriously on the mouldering walls. The iron hook in the oak beam, that crossed the ceiling midway, fascinated him, not with fear, but morbidly. So, it was from that hook that for twelve years, twelve long years of changing summer and winter, the body of Count Albert, murderer and suicide, hung in its strange casing of mediaeval steel; moving a little at first, and turning gently while the fire died out on the hearth, while the ruins of the castle grew cold, and horrified peasants sought for the bodies of the score of gay, reckless, wicked guests whom Count Albert had gathered in Kropfsberg for a last debauch, gathered to their terrible and untimely death. What a strange and fiendish idea it was, the young, handsome noble who had ruined himself and his family in the society of the splendid debauchees, gathering them all together, men and women who had known only love and pleasure, for a glorious and awful not of luxury, and then, when they were all dancing in the great ballroom, locking the doors and burning the whole castle about them, the while he sat in the great keep listening to their screams of agonized fear, watching the fire sweep from wing to wing until the whole mighty mass was one enormous and awful pyre, and. then, clothing himself in his great-great-grand-father's armor, hanging himself in the midst of the ruins of what had been a proud and noble castle. So ended a great family, a great house.

But that was forty years ago.

He was growing drowsy; the light flickered and flared in the fireplace; one by one the candles went out; the shadows grew thick in the room. Why did that great iron hook stand out so plainly? why did that dark shadow dance and quiver so mockingly behind it? —why — But he ceased to wonder at anything. He was asleep.

It seemed to him that he woke almost immediately; the fire still burned, though low and fitfully on the hearth. Otto was sleeping, breathing quietly and regularly; the shadows had gathered close around him, thick and murky; with every passing moment the light died in the fireplace; he felt stiff with cold. In the utter silence he heard the clock in the village strike two. He shivered with a sudden and irresistible feeling of fear, and abruptly turned and looked towards the hook in the ceiling.

Yes, It was there. He knew that It would be. It seemed quite natural, he would have been disappointed had he seen nothing; but now he knew that the story was true, knew that he was wrong, and that the dead _do_ sometimes return to earth, for there, in the fast-deepening shadow, hung the black mass of wrought steel, turning a little now and then, with the light flickering on the tarnished and rusty metal. He watched it quietly; he hardly felt afraid; it was rather a sentiment of sadness and fatality that filled him, of gloomy forebodings of something unknown, unimaginable. He sat and watched the thing disappear in the gathering dark, his hand on his pistol as it lay by him on the great chest. There was no sound but the regular breathing of the sleeping boy on the mattress.

It had grown absolutely dark; a bat fluttered against the broken glass of the window. He wondered if he was growing mad, for — he hesitated to acknowledge it to himself — he heard music; far, curious music, a strange and luxurious dance, very faint, very vague, but unmistakable.

Like a flash of lightning came a jagged line of fire down the blank wall opposite him, a line that remained, that grew wider, that let a pale cold light into the room, showing him now all its details, — the empty fireplace, where a thin smoke rose in a spiral from a bit of charred wood, the mass of the great bed, and, in the very middle, black against the curious brightness, the armored man, or ghost, or devil, standing, not suspended, beneath the rusty hook. And with the rending of the wall the music grew more distinct, though sounding still very, very far away.

Count Albert raised his mailed hand and beckoned to him; then turned, and stood in the riven wall.

Without a word, Rupert rose and followed him, his pistol in hand. Count Albert passed through the mighty wan and disappeared in the unearthly light. Rupert followed mechanically. He felt the crushing of the mortar beneath his feet, the roughness of the jagged wall where he rested his hand to steady himself.

The keep rose absolutely isolated among the ruins, yet on passing through the wall Rupert found himself in a long", uneven corridor, the floor of which was warped and sagging, while the walls were covered on one side with big faded portraits of an inferior quality, like those in the corridor that connects the Pitti and Uffizzi in Florence. Before him moved the figure of Count Albert, —a black silhouette in the ever-increasing light. And always the music grew stronger and stranger, a mad, evil, seductive dance that bewitched even while it disgusted.

In a final blaze of vivid, intolerable light, in a burst of hellish music that might have come from Bedlam, Rupert stepped from the corridor into a vast and curious room where at first he saw nothing, distinguished nothing but a mad, seething whirl of sweeping figures, white, in a white room, under white light, Count Albert standing before him, the only dark object to be seen. As his eyes grew accustomed to the fearful brightness, he knew that he was looking on a dance such as the damned might see in hell, but such as no living man had ever seen before.

Around the long, narrow hall, under the fearful light that came from nowhere, but was omnipresent, swept a rushing stream of unspeakable horrors, dancing insanely, laughing, gibbering hideously; the dead of forty years. White, polished skeletons, bare of flesh and vesture, skeletons clothed in the dreadful rags of dried and rattling sinews, the tags of tattering grave-clothes flaunting behind them. These were the dead of many years ago. Then the dead of more recent times, with yellow bones showing only here and there, the long and insecure hair of their hideous heads writhing in the beating air. Then green and gray horrors, bloated and shapeless, stained with earth or dripping with spattering water; and here and there white, beautiful things, like chiselled ivory, the dead of yesterday, locked it may be, in the mummy arms of rattling skeletons.

Round and round the cursed room, a swaying, swirling maelstrom of death, while the air grew thick with miasma, the floor foul with shreds of shrouds, and yellow parchment, clattering bones, and wisps of tangled hair.

And in the very midst of this ring of death, a sight not for words nor for thought, a sight to blast forever the mind of the man who looked upon it: a leaping, writhing dance of Count Albert's victims, the score of beautiful women and reckless men who danced to their awful death while the castle burned around them, charred and shapeless now, a living charnel-house of nameless horror.

Count Albert, who had stood silent and gloomy, watching the dance of the damned, turned to Rupert, and for the first time spoke.

"We are ready for you now; dance !

A prancing horror, dead some dozen years, perhaps, flaunted from the rushing river of the dead, and leered at Rupert with eyeless skull.

"Dance!"

Rupert stood frozen, motionless.

"Dance!"

His hard lips moved. "Not if the devil came from hell to make me.

Count Albert swept his vast two-handed sword into the foetid air while the tide of corruption paused in its swirling, and swept down on Rupert with gibbering grins.

The room, and the howling dead, and the black portent before him circled dizzily around, as with a last effort of departing consciousness he drew his pistol and fired full in the face of Count Albert.

Perfect silence, perfect darkness; not a breath, not a sound: the dead stillness of a long-sealed tomb. Rupert lay on his back, stunned, helpless, his pistol clenched in his frozen hand, a smell of powder in the black air. Where was he? Dead? In hell? He reached his hand out cautiously; it fell on dusty boards. Outside, far away, a clock struck three. Had he dreamed? Of course; but how ghastly a dream! With chattering teeth he called softly,—

"Otto !"

There was no reply, and none when he called again and again. He staggered weakly to his feet, groping for matches and candles. A panic of abject terror came on him; the matches were gone! He turned towards the fireplace: a single coal glowed in the white ashes. He swept a mass of papers and dusty books from the table, and with trembling hands cowered over the embers, until he succeeded in lighting the dry tinder. Then he piled the old books on the blaze, and looked fearfully around.

No: It was gone, — thank God for that; the hook was empty.

But why did Otto sleep so soundly; why did he not awake ?

He stepped unsteadily across the room in the flaring light of the burning books, and knelt by the mattress.

So they found him in the morning, when no one came to the inn from Kropfs-berg Keep, and the quaking Peter Rosskopf arranged a relief party; —found him kneeling beside the mattress where Otto lay, shot in the throat and quite dead.

THE WHITE VILLA

The White Villa

WHEN we left Naples on the 8.10 train for Paestum, Tom and I, we fully intended returning by the 2.46. Not because two hours time seemed enough wherein to exhaust the interests of those deathless ruins of a dead civilization, but simply for the reason that, as our _Indicatore_ informed us, there was but one other train, and that at 6.11, which would land us in Naples too late for the dinner at the Turners and the San Carlo afterwards. Not that I cared in the least for the dinner or the theatre; but then, I was not so obviously in Miss Turner's good graces as Tom Rendel was, which made a difference.

However, we had promised, so that was an end of it.

This was in the spring of '88, and at that time the railroad, which was being pushed onward to Reggio, whereby travellers to Sicily might be spared the agonies of a night on the fickle Mediterranean, reached no farther than Agropoli, some twenty miles beyond Paestum; but although the trains were as yet few and slow, we accepted the half-finished road with gratitude, for it penetrated the very centre of Campanian brigandage, and made it possible for us to see the matchless temples in safety, while a few years before it was necessary for intending visitors to obtain a military escort from the Government; and military escorts are not for young architects.

So we set off contentedly, that white May morning, determined to make the best of our few hours, little thinking that before we saw Naples again we were to witness things that perhaps no American had ever seen before.

For a moment, when we left the train at "Pesto," and started to walk up the flowery lane leading to the temples, we were almost inclined to curse this same railroad. We had thought, in our innocence, that we should be alone, that no one else would think of enduring the long four hours' ride from Naples just to spend two hours in the ruins of these temples; but the event proved our unwisdom. We were _not_ alone. It was a compact little party of conventional sight-seers that accompanied us. The inevitable English family with the three daughters, prominent of teeth, flowing of hair, aggressive of scarlet Murrays and Baedekers; the two blond and untidy Germans; a French couple from the pages of _La Vie Parisienne_; and our "old man of the sea," the white-bearded Presbyterian minister from Pennsylvania who had made our life miserable in Rome at the time of the Pope's Jubilee. Fortunately for us, this terrible old mart had fastened himself upon a party of American school-teachers travelling _en Cook_, and for the time we were safe; but our vision of two hours of dreamy solitude faded lamentably away.

Yet how beautiful it was! this golden meadow walled with far, violet mountains, breathless under a May sun; and in the midst, rising from tangles of asphodel and acanthus, vast in the vacant plain, three temples, one silver gray, one golden gray, and one flushed with intangible rose. And all around nothing but velvet meadows stretching from the dim mountains behind, away to the sea, that showed only as a thin line of silver just over the edge of the still grass.

The tide of tourists swept noisily through the Basilica and the temple of Poseidon across the meadow to the distant temple of Ceres, and Tom and I were left alone to drink in all the fine wine of dreams that was possible in the time left us. We gave but little space to examining the temples the tourists had left, but in a few moments found ourselves lying in the grass to the east of Poseidon, looking dimly out towards the sea, heard now, but not seen, — a vague and pulsating murmur that blended with the humming of bees all about us.

A small shepherd boy, with a woolly dog, made shy advances of friendship, and in a little time we had set him to gathering flowers for us: asphodels and bee-orchids, anemones, and the little thin green iris so fairylike and frail. The murmur of the tourist crowd had merged itself in the moan of the sea, and it was very still; suddenly I heard the words I had been waiting for, — the suggestion I had refrained from making myself, for I knew Thomas.

"I say, old man, shall we let the 2.46 go to thunder ?"

I chuckled to myself. "But the Turners?"

"They be blowed, we can tell them we missed the train."

"That is just exactly what we shall do," I said, pulling out my watch, unless we start for the station right now.

But Tom drew an acanthus leaf across his face and showed no signs of moving; so I filled my pipe again, and we missed the train.

As the sun dropped lower towards the sea, changing its silver line to gold, we pulled ourselves together, and for an hour or more sketched vigorously; but the mood was not on us. It was too jolly fine to waste time working, as Tom said; so we started off to explore the single street of the squalid town of Presto that was lost within the walls of dead Poseidonia. It was not a pretty village, — if you can call a rut-riven lane and a dozen houses a village,— nor were the inhabitants thereof reassuring in appearance. There was no sign of a church, — nothing but dirty huts, and in the midst, one of two stories, rejoicing in the name of _Albergo del Sole_, the first story of which was a black and cavernous smithy, where certain swarthy knaves, looking like banditti out of a job, sat smoking sulkily.

"We might stay here all night," said Tom, grinning askance at this choice company; but his suggestion was not received with enthusiasm.

Down where the lane from the station joined the main road stood the only sign of modern Civilization, — a great square structure, half villa, half fortress, with round turrets on its four corners, and a ten-foot wall surrounding it. There were no windows in its first story, so far as we could see, and it had evidently been at one time the fortified villa of some Campanian noble. Now, however, whether because brigandage had been stamped out, or because the villa was empty and deserted, it was no longer formidable; the gates of the great wall hung sagging on their hinges, brambles growing all over them, and many of the windows in the upper story were broken and black. It was a strange place, weird and mysterious, and we looked at it curiously. "There is a story about that place, said Tom, with conviction.

It was growing late: the sun was near the edge of the sea as we walked down the ivy-grown walls of the vanished city for the last time, and as we turned back, a red hush poured from the west, and painted the Doric temples in pallid rose against the evanescent purple of the Apennines. Already a thin mist was rising from the meadows, and the temples hung pink in the misty grayness. It was a sorrow to leave the beautiful things, but we could., run no risk of missing this last train, so we walked slowly back towards the temples.

What is that Johnny waving his arm at us for ?" asked Tom, suddenly.

"How should I know ? We are not on his land, and. the walls don't matter."

We pulled out our watches simultaneously.

"What time are you?" I said.

"Six minutes before six."

"And I am seven minutes. It can't take us all that time to walk to the station."

"Are you sure the train goes at 6.11 ?"

"Dead sure," I answered; and showed him the _Indicatore_.

By this time a woman and two children were shrieking at us hysterically; but what they said I had no idea, their Italian being of a strange and awful nature.

Look here, I said, " let's run; perhaps our watches are both slow."

"Or —perhaps the time-table is changed."

Then we ran, and the populace cheered and shouted with enthusiasm; our dignified run became a panic-stricken rout, for as we turned into the lane, smoke was rising from beyond the bank that hid the railroad; a bell rang; we were so near that we could hear the interrogative _Pronte_ ? the impatient _Partenza_ ? and the definitive _Andianio_! But the train was five hundred yards away, steaming towards Naples, when we plunged into the station as the clock struck six, and yelled for the station-master.

He came, and we indulged in crimination and recrimination.

When we could regard the situation calmly, it became apparent that the time-table _had_ been changed two days before, the 6.II now leaving at 5.58. A _facchino_ came in, and we four sat down and regarded the situation judicially.

"Was there any other train ?"

"No."

"Could we stay at the Albergo del Sole ?"

A forefinger drawn across the throat by the Capo Stazione with a significant "cluck" closed that question.

"Then we must stay with you here at the station."

"But, Signori, I am not married. I live here only with the _facchini_. I have only one room to sleep in. It is impossible !

"But we must sleep somewhere, likewise eat. What can we do ? and we shifted the responsibility deftly on the shoulders of the poor old man, who was growing excited again.

He trotted nervously up and. down the station for a minute, then he called the _facchino_. "Giuseppe, go up to the villa and ask if two _forestieri_ who have missed the last train can stay there all night!"

Protests were useless. The _facchino_ was gone, and we waited anxiously for his return. It seemed as though he would never come. Darkness had fallen, and the moon was rising over the mountains. At last he appeared.

"The Signori may stay all night, and welcome; but they cannot come to dinner, for there is nothing in the house to eat!"

This was not reassuring, and again the old station-master lost himself in meditation. The results were admirable, for in a little time the table in the waiting-room had been transformed into a dining-table, and Tom and I were ravenously devouring a big omelette, and bread and cheese, and drinking a most shocking sour wine as though it were Château Yquem. A _facchino_ served us, with clumsy good-will; and when we had induced our nervous old host to sit down with us and partake of his own hospitality, we succeeded in forming a passably jolly dinner-party, forgetting over our sour wine and cigarettes the coming hours from ten until sunrise, which lay rise, which lay before us in a dubious mist.

It was with crowding apprehensions which we strove in vain to joke away that we set out at last to retrace our steps to the mysterious villa, the _facchino_ Giuseppe leading the way. By this time the moon was well overhead, and just behind us as we tramped up the dewy lane, white in the moonlight between the ink-black hedgerows on either side. How still it was! Not a breath of air, not a sound of life; only the awful silence that had lain almost unbroken for two thousand years over this vast graveyard of a dead world.

As we passed between the shattered gates and wound our way in the moonlight through the maze of gnarled fruit-trees, decaying farm implements and piles of lumber, towards the small door that formed the only opening in the first story of this deserted fortress, the cold silence was shattered by the harsh baying of dogs somewhere in the distance to the right, beyond the barns that formed one side of the court. From the villa came neither light nor sound. Giuseppe knocked at the weather-worn door, and the sound echoed cavernously within; but there was no other reply. He knocked again and again, and at length we heard the rasping jar of sliding bolts, and the door opened a little, showing an old, old man, bent with age and gaunt with malaria. Over his head he held a big Roman lamp, with three wicks, that cast strange shadows on his face, — a face that was harmless in its senility, but intolerably sad. He made no reply to our timid salutations, but motioned tremblingly to us to enter; and with a last good-night to Giuseppe we obeyed, and stood half-way up the stone stairs that led directly from the door, while the old man tediously shot every bolt and adjusted the heavy bar.

Then we followed him in the semi-darkness up the steps into what had been the great hall of the villa. A fire was burning in a great fireplace so beautiful in design that Tom and I looked at each other with interest. By its fitful light we could see that we were in a huge circular room covered by a flat, saucer-shaped dome, — a room that must once have been superb and splendid, but that now was a lamentable wreck. The frescoes on the dome were stained and mildewed, and here and there the plaster was gone altogether; the carved doorways that led out on all sides had lost half the gold with which they had once been covered, and the floor was of brick, sunken into treacherous valleys. Rough chests, piles of old newspapers, fragments of harnesses, farm implements, a heap of rusty carbines and cutlasses, nameless litter of every possible kind, made the room into a wilderness which under the firelight seemed even more picturesque than it really was. And on this inexpressible confusion of lumber the pale shapes of the seventeenth-century nymphs, startling in the weather-stained nudity, looked down with vacant smiles.

For a few moments we warmed ourselves before the fire; and then, in the same dejected silence, the old man led the way to one of the many doors, handed us a brass lamp, and with a stiff bow turned his back on us.

Once in our room alone, Tom and I looked at each other with faces that expressed the most complex emotions.

"Well, of all the rum goes, said Tom, "this is the rummiest go I ever experienced!"

"Right, my boy; as you very justly remark, we are in for it. Help me shut this door, and then we will reconnoitre, take account of stock, and size up our chances."

But the door showed no sign of closing; it grated on the brick floor and stuck in the warped casing, and it took our united efforts to jam the two inches of oak into its place, and turn the enormous old key in its rusty lock.

"Better now, much better now, said Tom; "now let us see where we are."

The room was easily twenty-five feet square, and high in proportion; evidently it had been a state apartment, for the walls were covered with carved panelling that had once been white and gold, with mirrors in the panels, the wood now stained every imaginable color, the mirrors cracked and broken, and dull with mildew. A big fire had just been lighted in the fireplace, the shutters were closed, and although the only furniture consisted of two massive bedsteads, and a chair with one leg shorter than the others, the room seemed almost comfortable.

I opened one of the shutters, that closed the great windows that ran from the floor almost to the ceiling, and nearly fell through the cracked glass into the floorless balcony. "Tom, come here, quick," I cried; and for a few minutes neither of us thought about our dubious surroundings, for we were looking at Paestum by moonlight.

A flat, white mist, like water, lay over the entire meadow; from the midst rose against the blue-black sky the three ghostly temples, black and silver in the vivid moonlight, floating, it seemed, in the fog; and behind them, seen in broken glints between the pallid shafts, stretched the line of the silver sea.

Perfect silence,—the silence of implacable death.

We watched the white tide of mist rise around the temples, until we were chilled through, and so presently went to bed. There was but one door in the room, and that was securely locked; the great windows were twenty feet from the ground, so we felt reasonably safe from all possible attack.

In a few minutes Tom was asleep and breathing audibly; but my constitution is more nervous than his, and I lay awake for some little time, thinking of our curious adventure and of its possible outcome. Finally, I fell asleep, — for how long I do not know: but I woke with the feeling that some one had tried the handle of the door. The fire had fallen into a heap of coals which cast a red glow in the room, whereby I could see dimly the outline of Tom's bed, the broken-legged chair in front of the fireplace, and the door in its deep casing by the chimney, directly in front of my bed. I sat up, nervous from my sudden awakening under these strange circumstances, and stared at the door. The latch rattled, and the door swung smoothly open. I began to shiver coldly. That door was locked; Tom and I had all we could do to jam it together and lock it. But we _did_ lock it; and now it was opening silently. In a minute more it as silently closed.

Then I heard a footstep, — I swear I heard a footstep _in the room_, and with it the _frou-frou_ of trailing skirts; my breath stopped and my teeth grated against each other as I heard the soft footfalls and the feminine rustle pass along the room towards the fireplace. My eyes saw nothing; yet there was enough light in the room for me to distinguish the pattern on the carved panels of the door. The steps stopped by the fire, and I saw the broken-legged chair lean to the left, with a little jar as its short leg touched the floor.

I sat still, frozen, motionless, staring at the vacancy that was filled with such terror for me; and as I looked, the seat of the chair creaked, and it came back to its upright position again.

And then the footsteps came down the room lightly, towards the window; there was a pause, and then the great shutters swung back, and the white moonlight poured in. Its brilliancy was unbroken by any shadow, by any sign of material substance.

I tried to cry out, to make some sound, to awaken Tom; this sense of utter loneliness in the presence of the Inexplicable was maddening. I don't know whether my lips obeyed my will or no; at all events, Tom lay motionless, with his deaf ear up, and gave no sign.

The shutters closed as silently as they had opened; the moonlight was gone, the firelight also, and in utter darkness I waited. If I could only _see_! If something were visible, I should not mind it so much; but this ghastly hearing of every little sound, every rustle of a gown, every breath, yet seeing nothing, was soul-destroying. I think in my abject terror I prayed that I might see, only see; but the darkness was unbroken.

Then the footsteps began to waver fitfully, and I heard the rustle of garments sliding to the floor, the clatter of little shoes flung down, the rattle of buttons, and of metal against wood.

Rigors shot over me, and my whole body shivered with collapse as I sank back on the pillow, waning with every nerve tense, listening with all my life.

The coverlid was turned back beside me, and in another moment the great bed sank a little as something slipped between the sheets with an audible sigh.

I called to my aid every atom of remaining strength, and, with a cry that shivered between my clattering teeth, I hurled myself headlong from the bed on to the floor.

I must have lain for some time stunned and unconscious, for when I finally came to myself it was cold in the room, there was no last glow of lingering coals in the fireplace, and I was stiff with chill.

It all Hashed over me like the haunting of a heavy dream. I laughed a little at the dim memory, with the thought, "I must try to recollect all the details; they win do to ten 10m, and rose stiffly to return to bed, when—-there it was again, and my heart stopped, —the hand on the door.

I paused and listened. The door opened with a muffled creak, closed again, and I heard the lock turn rustily. I would have died now before getting into that bed again; but there was terror equally without; so I stood trembling and listened, — listened to heavy, stealthy steps creeping along on the other side of the bed. I clutched the coverlid, staring across into the dark.

There was a rush in the air by my face, the sound of a blow, and simultaneously a shriek, so awful, so despairing, so blood-curdling that felt my senses leaving me again as I sank crouching on the floor by the bed.

And then began the awful duel, the duel of invisible, audible shapes; of things that shrieked and raved, mingling thin, feminine cries with low, stifled curses and indistinguishable words. Round and round the room, foot-steps chasing footsteps in the ghastly night, now away by Tom's bed, now rushing swiftly down the great room until I felt the flash of swirling drapery on my hard lips. Round and round, turning and twisting till my brain whirled with the mad cries.

They were coming nearer. I felt the jar of their feet on the floor beside me. Came one long, gurgling moan close over my head, and then, crushing down upon me, the weight of a collapsing body; there was long hair over my face, and in my staring eyes; and as awful silence succeeded the less awful tumult, life went out, and I fell unfathomable miles into nothingness.

The gray dawn was sifting through the chinks in the shutters when I opened my eyes again. I lay stunned and faint, staring up at the mouldy frescoes on the ceil-

ing, struggling to gather together my wandering senses and knit them into something like consciousness. But now as I pulled myself little by little together there
was no thought of dreams before me. One after another the awful incidents of that
un-speakarue night came back, and I lay incapable of movement, of action, trying to
piece together the winning fragments of memory that circled dizzily around me.

Little by little it grew lighter in the room. I could see the pallid lines struggling
through the shutters behind me, grow stronger along the broken and dusty floor.
The tarnished mirrors reflected dirtily the growing daylight; a door closed, far away,
and I heard the crowing of a cock; then by and by the whistle of a passing train.

Years seemed to have passed since I first came into this terrible room. I had
lost the use of my tongue, my voice refused to obey my panic-stricken desire to cry
out; once or twice I tried in vain to force an articulate sound through my rigid lips;
and when at last a broken whisper rewarded my feverish struggles, I felt a strange
sense of great victory. How soundly he slept! Ordinarily, rousing mm was no easy
task, and now he revolted steadily against being awakened at this untimely hour. It
seemed to me that I had called him for ages almost, before I heard him grunt sleep-
ily and turn in bed.

"Tom," I cried weakly, "Tom, come and help me!"

"What do you want ? what is the matter with
you?"

"Don't ask, come and help me !"

"Fallen out of bed I guess;" and he laughed drowsily.

My abject terror lest he should go to sleep again gave me new strength. Was
it the actual physical paralysis born of killing fear that held me down ? I could not
have raised my head from the floor on my life; I could only cry out in deadly fear
for Tom to come and help me.

"Why don't you get up and get into bed?" he answered, when I implored him to come to me. "You have got a bad nightmare; wake up!"

But something in my voice roused him at last, and he came chuckling across the room, stopping to throw open two of the great shutters and let a burst of white light into the room. He climbed upon the bed and peered over jeeringly. With the first glance the laugh died, and he leaped the bed and bent over me.

"My God, man, what is the matter with you? You are hurt!

"I don't know what is the matter; lift me up, get me away from here, and I 11 tell you all I know."

"But, old chap, you must be hurt awfully; the floor is covered with blood !

He lifted my head and held me in his powerful arms. I looked down: a great red stain blotted the floor beside me.

But, apart from the black bruise on my head, there was no sign of a wound on my body, nor stain of blood on my lips. In as few words as possible I told him the whole story.

"Let's get out of this," he said when I had finished; this is no place for us. Brigands I can stand, but—"

He helped me to dress, and as soon as possible we forced open the heavy door, the door I had seen turn so softly on its hinges only a few hours before, and came out into the great circular hall, no less strange and mysterious now in the half light of dawn than it had been by firelight. The room was empty, for it must have been very early, although a fire already blazed in the fireplace. We sat by the fire some time, seeing no one. Presently slow footsteps sounded in the stairway, and the old man entered, silent as the night before, nodding to us civilly, but showing by no sign any surprise which he may have felt at our early rising. In absolute silence he moved around, preparing coffee for us; and when at last the frugal breakfast was ready, and we sat around the rough table munching coarse bread and sipping the black coffee, he would reply to our overtures only by monosyllables.

Any attempt at drawing from him some facts as to the history of the villa was received with a grave and frigid repellence that baffled us; and we were forced to say _addio_with our hunger for some explanation of the events of the night still unsatisfied.

But we saw the temples by sunrise, when the mistlike lambent opals bathed the bases of the tall columns salmon in the morning light! It was a rhapsody in the pale and unearthly colors of Puvis de Chavannes vitalized and made glorious with splendid sunlight; the apotheosis of mist; a vision never before seen, never to be forgotten. It was so beautiful that the memory of my ghastly night paled and faded, and it was Tom who assailed the station-master with questions while we waited for the train from Agropoli.

Luckily he was more than loquacious, he was voluble under the ameliorating influence of the money we forced upon him; and this, in few words, was the story he told us while we sat on me platform smoking, marvelling at the mists that rose to the east, now veiling, now revealing the lavender Apennines.

"Is there a story of __La Villa Biance ?"_

"Ah, Signori, certainly; and a story very strange and very terrible. It was much time ago, a hundred, — two hundred years; I do not know. Well, the Duca di San Damiano married a lady so fair, so most beautiful that she was called _La Luna di Pesto_; but she was of the people, — more, she was of the banditti: her father was of Calabria, and a terror of the Campagna. But the Duke was young, and he married her, and for her built the white villa; and it was a wonder throughout Campania, — you have seen? It is splendid now, even if a ruin. Well, it was less than a year after they came to the villa before the Duke grew jealous, — jealous of the new captain of the banditti who took the place of the father of _La Luna,_ himself killed in a great battle up there in the mountains. Was there cause ? Who shall know ? But there were stones among the people of terrible things in the villa, and how _La Lima_ was seen almost never outside the walls. Then the Duke would go for many days to Napoli, coming home only now and then to the villa that was become a fortress, so many men guarded its never-opening gates. And once—it was in the spring—the Duke came silently down from Napoli, and there, by the three poplars you see away towards the north, his carriage was set upon by armed men, and he was almost killed; but he had with him many guards, and after a terrible fight the brigands were beaten off; but before him, wounded, lay the captain, — the man whom he feared and hated. He looked at him, lying there under the torchlight, and in his hand _saw his own sword_. Then he became a devil: with the same sword he ran the brigand through, leaped in the carriage, and, entering the villa, crept to the chamber of _La Luna_, and killed her with the sword she had given to her lover.

"This is all the story of the White Villa, except that the Duke came never again to Pesto. He went back to the king at Napoli, and for many years he was the scourge of the banditti of Campania; for the King made him a general, and San Damiano was a name feared by the lawless and loved by the peaceful, until he was killed in a battle down by Mormanno.

"And _La Luna_? Some say she comes back to the villa, once a year, when the moon is full, in the month when she was slain; for the Duke buried her, they say, with his own hands, in the garden that was once under the window of her chamber; and as she died unshriven, so was she buried without the pale of the Church. Therefore she cannot sleep in peace, — _non è vero_ ? I do not know if the story is true, but this is the story, Signori, and there is the train for Napoli. _Ah, grazie! Signori, graziè tanto! A rive-derci! Signori, a rivederci!"_

SISTER MADDELENA

ACROSS the valley of the Oreto from Monreale, on the slopes of the mountains just above the little village of Parco, lies the old convent of Sta. Catarina. From the cloister terrace at Monreale you can see its pale walls and the slim campanile of its chapel rising from the crowded citron and mulberry orchards that flourish, rank and wild, no longer cared for by pious and loving hands. From the rough road that climbs the mountains to Assunto, the convent is invisible, a gnarled and ragged olive grove intervening, and a spur of cliffs as well, while from Palermo one sees only the speck of white, flashing in the sun, indistinguishable from the many similar gleams of desert monastery or pauper village.

Partly because of this seclusion, partly by reason of its extreme beauty, partly, it may be, because the present owners are more than charming and gracious in their pressing hospitality, Sta. Catarina seems to preserve an element of the poetic, almost magical; and as I drove with the Cavaliere Valguanera one evening in March out of Palermo, along the garden valley of the Oreto, then up the mountain side where the warm light of the spring sunset swept across from Monreale, lying golden and mellow on the luxuriant growth of figs, and olives, and orange-trees, and fantastic cacti, and so up to where the path of the convent swung off to the right round a dizzy point of cliff that reached out gaunt and gray from the olives below, — as I drove thus in the balmy air, and saw of a sudden a vision of creamy walls and orange roofs, draped in fantastic festoons of roses, with a single curving palm-tree stuck black and feathery against the gold sunset, it is hardly to be wondered at that I should slip into a mood of visionary enjoyment, looking for a time on the whole thing as the misty phantasm of a summer dream.

The Cavaliere had introduced himself to us, — Tom Rendel and me, — one morning soon after we reached Palermo, when, in the first bewilderment of architects in this paradise of art and color, we were working nobly at our sketches in that dream of delight, the Capella Palatina. He was himself an amateur archaeologist, he told us, and passionately devoted to his island; so he felt impelled to speak to any one whom he saw appreciating the almost—and in a way fortunately — unknown beauties of Palermo. In a little time we were fully acquainted, and talking like the oldest friends. Of course he knew acquaintances of Rendel's, — some one always does: this time they were officers on the tubby U. S. S. "Quinebaug," that, during the summer of 1888, was trying to uphold the maritime honor of the United

States in European waters. Luckily for us, one of the officers was a kind of cousin of Rendel's, and came from Baltimore as well, so, as he had visited at the Cavaliere's place, we were soon invited to do the same. It was in this way that, with the luck that attends Rendel wherever he goes, we came to see something of domestic life in Italy, and that I found myself involved in another of those adventures for which I naturally sought so little.

I wonder if there is any other place in Sicily so faultless as Sta. Catarina? Taormina is a paradise, an epitome of all that is beautiful in Italy, — Venice excepted. Girgenti is a solemn epic, with its golden temples between the sea and hills. Cefalú is wild and strange, and Monreale a vision out of a fairy tale; but Sta. Catarina! —

Fancy a convent of creamy stone and. rose-red brick perched on a ledge of rock midway between earth and heaven, the cliff falling almost sheer to the valley two hundred feet and more, the mountain rising behind straight towards the sky; all the rocks covered with cactus and dwarf fig-trees, the convent draped in smothering roses, and in front a terrace with a fountain in the midst; and then — nothing — between you and the sapphire sea, six miles away. Below stretches the Eden valley, the Concha d'Oro, gold-green fig orchards alternating with smoke-blue olives, the mountains rising on either hand and sinking undulously away towards the bay where, like a magic city of ivory and nacre, Palermo lies guarded by the twin mountains, Monte Pelligrino and Capo Zafferano arid rocks like dull amethysts, rose in sunlight, violet in shadow: lions couchant,guarding the sleeping town.

Seen as we saw it for the first time that hot evening in March, with the golden lambent light pouring down through the valley, making it in verity a "shell of gold," sitting in Indian chairs on the terrace, with the perfume of roses and jasmines all around us, the valley of the Oreto, Palermo, Sta. Catarina, Monreale, all were but parts of a dreamy vision, like the heavenly city of Sir Percivale, to attain which he passed across the golden bridge that burned after him as he vanished in the intolerable light of the Beatific Vision.

It was all so unreal, so phantasmal, that I was not surprised in the least when, late in the evening after the ladies had gone to their rooms, and the Cavaliere, Tom, and I were stretched out in chairs on the terrace, smoking lazily under the multitudinous stars, the Cavaliere said, "There is something I really must tell you both before you go to bed, so that you may be spared any unnecessary alarm."

"You are going to say that the place is haunted," said Rendel, feeling vaguely on the floor beside him for his glass of Amaro: "thank you; it is all its needs."

The Cavaliere smiled a little: "Yes, that is just it. Sta. Catarina is really haunted; and much as my reason revolts against the idea as superstitious and savoring of priestcraft, yet I must acknowledge I see no way of avoiding the admission. I do not presume to offer any explanations, I only state the fact; and the fact is that to-night one or other of you will, in all human — or unhuman—probability, receive a visit from Sister Maddelena. You need not be in the east afraid, the apparition is perfectly gentle and harmless; and, moreover, having seen it once, you will never see it again. No one sees the ghost, or whatever it is, but once, and that usually the first night he spends in the house. I myself saw the thing eight — nine years ago, when I first bought the place from the Marchese di Muxaro; all my people have seen it, nearly all my guests, so I think you may as well be prepared."

"Then tell us what to expect," I said; "what kind of a ghost is this nocturnal visitor ?"

"It is simple enough. Some time to-night you will suddenly awake and see before you a Carmelite nun who will look fixedly at you, say distinctly and very sadly, ' I cannot sleep,' and then vanish. That is all, it is hardly worth speaking of, only some people are terribly frightened if they are visited unwarned by strange apparitions; so I tell you this that you may be prepared.

"This was a Carmelite convent, then ?" I said.

"Yes; it was suppressed after the unification of Italy, and given to the House of Muxaro; but the family died out, and I bought it. There is a story about the ghostly nun, who was only a novice, and even that unwillingly, which gives an interest to an otherwise very commonplace and uninteresting ghost."

"I beg that you will tell it us," cried Rendel.

"There is a storm coming," I added, "See, the lightning is flashing already up among the mountains at the head of the valley; if the story is tragic, as it must be, now is just the time for it. You will tell it, will you not?

The Cavaliere smiled that slow, cryptic smile of his that was so unfathomable.

"As you say, there is a shower coming, and as we have fierce tempests here, we might not sleep; so perhaps we may as well sit up a little longer, and I will tell you the story."

The air was utterly still, hot and oppressive; the rich, sick odor of the oranges just bursting into bloom came up from the valley in a gently rising tide. The sky, thick with stars, seemed mirrored in the rich foliage below, so numerous were the glow-worms under the still trees, and the fireflies that gleamed in the hot air. Lightning flashed fitfully from the darkening west; but as yet no thunder broke the heavy silence.

The Cavaliere lighted another cigar, and pulled a cushion under his head so that he could look down to the distant lights of the city. "This is the story," he said.

"Once upon a time, late in the last century, the Duca di Castiglione was attached to the court of Charles III., King of the Two Sicilies, down at Palermo. They tell me he was very ambitious, and, not content with marrying his son to one of the ladies of the House of Tuscany, had betrothed his only daughter, Rosalia, to Prince Antonio, a cousin of the king. His whole life was wrapped up in the fame of his family, and he quite forgot all domestic affection in his madness for dynastic glory. His son was a worthy scion, cold and proud; but Rosalia was, according to legend, utterly the reverse, — a passionate, beautiful girl, wilful and headstrong, and careless of her family and the world.

"The time had nearly come for her to marry Prince Antonio, a typical _roue_ of the Spanish court, when, through the treachery of a servant, the Duke discovered that his daughter was in love with a young military officer whose name I don't remember, and that an elopement had been planned to take place the next night. The fury and dismay of the old autocrat passed belief; he saw in a flash the downfall of all his hopes of family aggrandizement through union with the royal house, and, knowing well the spirit of his daughter, despaired of ever bringing her to subjection. Nevertheless, he attacked her unmercifully, and, by bullying and teats, by imprisonment, and even bodily chastisement, he tried to break her spirit and bend her to his indomitable will. Through his power at court he had the lover sent away to the mainland, and for more than a year he held daughter closely imprisoned in his palace on the Toledo, that one, you may remember, on the right, just beyond the Via del Collegio dei Gesuiti, with the beautiful iron-work grilles at all the windows, and the painted frieze.

But nothing could move her, nothing bend her stubborn will; and at last, furious at the girl he could not govern, Castiglione sent her to this convent, then one of the few houses of barefoot Carmelite nuns in Italy. He stipulated that she should take the name of Maddelena, that he should never hear of her again, and that she should be held an absolute prisoner in this conventual castle.

"Rosalia— or Sister Maddelena, as she was now— believed her lover dead, for her father had given her good proofs of this, and she believed him; nevertheless she refused to marry another, and seized upon the convent life as a blessed relief from the tyranny of her maniacal father.

"She lived here for four or five years; her name was forgotten at court and in her father's palace. Rosalia di Castiglione was dead, and only Sister Maddelena lived, a Carmelite nun, in her place.

"In 1798 Ferdinand IV. found himself driven from his throne on the mainland, his kingdom divided, and he himself forced to nee to Sicily. With him came the lover of the dead Rosalia, now high in military honor. He on his part had thought Rosalia dead, and it was only by accident that he found that she still lived, a Carmelite nun. Then began the second act of the romance that until then had been only sadly commonplace, but now became dark and tragic. Michele — Michele Biscari, — that was his name; I remember now — haunted the region of the convent, striving to communicate with Sister Maddelena; and at last, from the cliffs over us, up there among the citrons — you will see by the next flash of lightning — he saw her in the great cloister, recognized her in her white habit, found her the same dark and splendid beauty of six years before, only made more beautiful by her white habit and her rigid life. By and by he found a day when she was alone, and tossed a ring to her as she stood in the midst of the cloister. She looked up, saw him, and from that moment lived only to love him in life as she had loved his memory in the death she had thought had overtaken him.

"With the utmost craft they arranged their plans together. They could not speak, for a word would have aroused the other inmates of the convent. They could make signs only when Sister Maddelena was alone. Michele could throw notes to her from the cliff, — a feat demanding a strong arm, as you will see, if you measure the distance with your eye, — and she could drop replies from the window over the cliff, which he picked up at the bottom. Finally he succeeded in casting into the cloister a coil of light rope. The girl fastened it to the bars of one of the windows, and — so great is the madness of love — Biscari actually climbed the rope from the valley to the window of the cell, a distance of almost two hundred feet, with but three little craggy resting-places in all that height. For nearly a month these nocturnal visits were undiscovered, and Michele had almost completed his arrangements for carrying the girl from Sta. Catarina and away to Spam, when unfortunately one of the some mystery, from the changed face of Sister Maddelena, began investigating, and at length discovered the rope neatly coiled up by the nun's window, and hidden under some clinging vines. She instantly told the Mother Superior; and together they watched from a window in the crypt of the chapel, — the only place, as you will see to-morrow, from which one could see the window of Sister Maddelena's cell. They saw the figure of Michele daringly ascending the slim rope; watched hour after hour, the Sister remaining while the Superior went to say the hours in the chapel, at each of which Sister Maddelena was present; and at last, at prime, just as the sun was rising, they saw the figure slip down the rope, watched the rope drawn up and concealed, and knew that Sister Maddelena was m their hands for vengeance and punishment, — a criminal.

"The next day, by the order of the Mother Superior, Sister Maddelena was imprisoned in one of the cells under the chapel, charged with her guilt, and commanded to make full and complete confession. But not a word would she say, although they offered her forgiveness if she would tell the name of her lover. At last the Superior told her that after this fashion would they act the coming night: she herself would be placed in the crypt, tied in front of the window, her mouth gagged; that the rope would be lowered, and the lover allowed to approach even to the sill of her window, and at that moment the rope would be cut, and before her eyes her lover would be dashed to death on the ragged cliffs. The plan was feasible, and Sister Maddelena knew that the Mother was perfectly capable of carrying it out. Her stubborn spirit was broken, and in the only- way possible; she begged for mercy, for the sparing of her lover. The Mother Superior was deaf at first; at last she said, 'It is your life or his. I will spare him on condition that you sacrifice your own life.' Sister Maddelena accepted the terms joyfully, wrote a last farewell to Michele, fastened the note to the rope, and with her own hands cut the rope and saw it fall coiling down to the valley bed far below.

"Then she silently prepared for death; and at midnight, while her lover was wandering, mad with the horror of impotent fear, around the white walls of the convent, Sister Maddelena, for love of Michele, gave up her life. How, was never known. That she was indeed dead was only a suspicion, for when Biscari finally compelled the civil authorities to enter the convent, claiming that murder had been done there, they found no sign. Sister Maddelena had been sent to the parent house of the barefoot Carmelites at Avila in Spain, so the Superior stated, because of her incorrigible contumacy. The old Duke of Castiglione refused to stir hand or foot in the matter, and Michele, after fruitless attempts to prove that the Superior of Sta. Catarina had caused the death, was forced to leave Sicily. He sought in Spain for very long; but no sign of the girl was to be found, and at last he died, exhausted with suffering and sorrow.

"Even the name of Sister Maddelena was forgotten, and it was not until the convents were suppressed, and this house came into the hands of the Muxaros, that her story was remembered. It was then that the ghost began to appear; and, an explanation being necessary, the story, or legend, was obtained from one of the nuns who still lived after the suppression. I think the fact — for it is a fact — of the ghost rather goes to prove that Michele was right, and that poor Rosalia gave her life a sacrifice for love, —whether in accordance with the terms of the legend or not, I cannot say. One or the other of you will probably see her to-night. You might ask her for the facts. Well, that is all the story of Sister Maddelena, known in the world as Rosalia di Castiglione. Do you like it ?"

"It is admirable,' said Rendel, enthusiastically. "But I fancy I should rather look on it simply as a story, and not as a warning of what is going to happen. I don't much fancy real ghosts myself."

"But the poor Sister is quite harmless; and valguanera rose, stretching himself. My servants say she wants a mass said over her, or something of that kind; but I haven't much love for such priestly hocus-pocus, — I beg your pardon (turning to me), "I had forgotten that you were a Catholic: forgive my rudeness.

"My dear Cavaliere, I beg you not to apologize. I am sorry you cannot see things as I do; but don't for a moment think I am hypersensitive."

"I have an excuse, perhaps you will say only an explanation; but I live where I see all the absurdities and corruptions of the Church.

"Perhaps you let the accidents blind you to the essentials; but do not let us quarrel to-night, — see, the storm is close on us. Shall we go in ?

The stars were blotted out through nearly all the sky; low, thunderous clouds, massed at the head of the valley, were sweeping over so close that they seemed to brush the black pines on the mountain above us. To the south and east the storm-clouds had shut down almost to the sea, leaving a space of black sky where the moon in its last quarter was rising just to the left of Monte Pellegrino, — a black silhouette against the pallid moonlight. The rosy lightning flashed almost incessantly, and through the fitful darkness came the sound of bells across the valley, the rushing torrent below, and the dull roar of the approaching rain, with a deep organ point of solemn thunder through it all.

We fled indoors from the coming tempest, and taking our candles, said "good-night," and sought each his respective room.

My own was in the southern part of the old convent, giving on the terrace we had just quitted, and about over the main doorway. The rushing storm, as it swept down the valley with the swelling torrent beneath, was very fascinating, and after wrapping myself in a dressing-gown I stood for some time by the deeply embrasured window, watching the blazing lightning and the beating rain whirled by fitful gusts of wind around the spurs of the mountains. Gradually the violence of the shower seemed to decrease, and I threw myself down on my bed in the hot air, wondering if I really was to experience the ghostly visit the Cavaliere so confidently predicted.

I had thought out the whole matter to my own satisfaction, and fancied I knew exactly what I should do, in case Sister Maddelena came to visit me. The story touched me: the thought of the poor faithful girl who sacrificed herself for her lover, — himself, very likely, quite unworthy, and who now could never sleep for reason of her unquiet soul, sent out into the storm of eternity without spiritual aid or counsel. I could not sleep; for the still vivid lightning, the crowding thoughts of the dead nun, and the shivering anticipation of my possible visitation, made slumber quite out of the question. No suspicion of sleepiness had visited me, when, perhaps an hour after midnight, came a sudden vivid flash of lightning, and, as my dazzled eyes began to regain the power of sight, I saw her as plainly as in life,—a tall figure, shrouded in the white habit of the Carmelites, her head bent, her hands clasped before her. In another hash of lightning she slowly raised her head and looked at me long and earnestly. She was very beautiful, like the Virgin of Beltraffio in the National Gallery, — more beautiful than I had supposed possible, her deep, passionate eyes very tender and pitiful in their pleading, beseeching glance. I hardly think I was frightened, or even startled, but lay looking steadily at her as she stood in the beating lighting.

Then she breathed, rather than articulated, with a voice that almost brought tears, so infinitely sad and sorrowful was it, "I cannot sleep!" and the liquid eyes grew more pitiful and questioning as bright tears fell from them down the pale dark face.

The figure began to move slowly towards the door, its eyes fixed on mine with a look that was weary and almost agonized. I leaped from the bed and stood waiting. A look of utter gratitude swept over the face, and, turning, the figure passed through the doorway.

Out into the shadow of the corridor it moved, like a drift of pallid storm-cloud, and I followed, all natural and instinctive fear or nervousness quite blotted out by the part I felt I was to play in giving rest to a tortured soul. The corridors were velvet black; but the pale figure floated before me always, an unerring guide, now but a thin mist on the utter night, now white and clear in the bluish lightning through some window or doorway.

Down the stairway into the lower hall, across the refectory, where the great frescoed Crucifixion flared into sudden clearness under the fit-ful lightning, out into the silent cloister.

It was very dark. I stumbled along the heaving bricks, now guiding myself by a hand on the whitewashed wall, row by a touch on a column wet with the storm. From all the eaves the rain was dripping on to the pebbles at the foot of the arcade: a pigeon, startled from the capital where it was sleeping, beat its way into the cloister close. Still the white thing drifted before me to the farther side of the court, then along the cloister at right angles, and paused before one of the many doorways that led to the cells.

A sudden blaze of fierce lightning, the last now of the fleeting trail of storm, leaped around us, and in the vivid light I saw the white face turned again with the look of overwhelming desire, of beseeching pathos, that had choked my throat with an involuntary sob when first I saw Sister Maddelena. In the brief interval that ensued after the hash, and before the roaring thunder burst like the crash of battle over the trembling convent, I heard again the sorrowful words, "I cannot sleep, come from the from penetrable darkness. And when the lightning came again, the white figure was gone.

I wandered around the courtyard, searching in vain for Sister Maddelena, even until the moonlight broke through the torn and sweeping fringes of the storm. I tried the door where the white figure vanished: it was locked; but I had found what I sought, and, carefully noting its location, went back to my room, but not to sleep.

In the morning the Cavaliere asked Rendel and me which of us had seen the ghost, and I told him my story; then I asked him to grant me permission to sift the thing to the bottom; and he courteously gave the whole matter into my charge, promising that he would consent to anything.

I could hardly wait to finish breakfast; but no sooner was this done than, forgetting my morning pipe, I started with Rendel and the Cavaliere to investigate.

"I am sure there is nothing in that cell," said Valguanera, when we came in front of the door I had marked. "It is curious that you should have chosen the door of the very cell that tradition assigns to Sister Maddelena; but I have often examined that room myself, and I am sure that there is no chance for anything to be concealed. In fact, I had the floor taken up once, soon after I came here, knowing the room was that of the mysterious Sister, and thinking that there, if anywhere, the monastic crime would have taken place; still, we will go in, if you like."

He unlocked the door, and we entered, one of is, at all events, with a beating heart. The cell was very small, hardly eight feet square. There certainly seemed no opportunity for concealing a body in the tiny place; and although I sounded the floor and walls, all gave a solid, heavy answer, — the unmistakable sound of masonry.

For the innocence of the floor the Cavaliere answered. He had, he said, had it all removed, even to the curving surfaces of the vault below; yet somewhere in this room the body of the murdered girl was concealed, — of this I was certain. But where? There seemed no answer; and I was compelled to give up the search for the moment, somewhat to the amusement of Valguanera, who had watched curiously to see if I could solve the mystery.

But I could not forget the subject, and towards noon started on another tour of investigation. I procured the keys from the Cavalliere, and examined the cells adjoining; they were apparently the same, each with its window opposite the door, and nothing Stay, were they the same ? I hastened into the suspected cell; it was as I thought: this cell, being on the corner, could have had two windows, yet only one was visible, and that to the left, at right angles with the doorway. Was it imagination ? As I sounded the wall opposite the door, where the other window should be, I fancied that the sound was a trifle less solid and dull. I was becoming excited. I dashed back to the cell on the right, and, forcing open the little window, thrust my head out.

It was found at last ! In the smooth surface of the yellow wall was a rough space, following approximately the shape of the other cell windows, not plastered like the rest of the wall, but showing the shapes of bricks through its thick coatings of whitewash. I turned with a gasp of excitement and satisfaction: yes, the embrasure of the wall was deep enough; what a wall it was ! — four feet at least, and the opening of the window reached to the floor, though the window itself was hardly three feet square. I felt absolutely certain that the secret was solved, and called the Cavaliere and Rendel, too excited to give them an explanation of my theories.

They must have thought me mad when I suddenly began scraping away at the solid wall in front of the door; but in a few minutes they understood what I was about, for under the coatings of paint and plaster appeared the original bricks; and as my architectural knowledge had led me rightly, the space I had cleared was directly over a vertical joint between firm, workmanlike masonry on one hand, and rough amateurish work on the other, bricks laid anyway, and without order or science.

Rendel seized a pick, and was about to assail the rude wall, when I stopped him.

"Let us be careful," I said; "who knows what we may find ? So we set to work digging out the mortar around a brick at about the level of our eyes.

How hard the mortar had become! But a brick yielded at last, and with trembling fingers I detached it. Darkness within, yet beyond question there was a cavity there, not a solid wall; and with infinite care we removed another brick. Still the hole was too small to admit enough light from the dimly illuminated cell. With a chisel we pried at the sides of a large block of masonry, perhaps eight bricks in size. It moved, and we softly slid it from its bed.

Valguanero, who was standing watching us as we lowered the bricks to the floor, gave a sudden cry, a cry like that of a frightened woman, — terrible, coming from him. Yet there was cause.

Framed by the ragged opening of the bricks, hardly seen in the dim light, was a face, an ivory image, more beautiful than any antique bust, but drawn and distorted by unspeakable agony: the lovely mouth half open, as though gasping for breath; the eyes cast upward; and below, slim chiselled hands crossed on the breast, but clutching the folds of the white Carmelite habit, torture and agony visible in every tense muscle, fighting against the determination of the rigid pose.

We stood there breathless, staring at the pitiful sight, fascinated, bewitched. So this was the secret. With fiendish ingenuity, the rigid ecclesiastics had blocked up the window, then forced the beautiful creature to stand in the alcove, while with remorseless hands and iron hearts they had shut her into a living tomb. I had read of such things in romance; but to find the verity here, before my eyes—

Steps came down the cloister, and with a simultaneous thought we sprang to the door and closed it behind us. The room was sacred; that awful sight was not for curious eyes. The gardener was coming to ask some trivial question of Valguanera. The Cavaliere cut him short. "Pietro, go down to Parco and ask Padre Stefano to come here at once. (I thanked him with a glance.) "Stay ! "He turned to me: "Signore, it is already two o'clock and too late for mass, is it not ?

I nodded.

Valguanera thought a moment, then he said, "Bring two horses; the Signer Americano will go with you, do you understand?" Then, turning to me, You will go, will you not? I think you can explain matters to Padre Stefano better than I."

"Of course I will go, more than gladly." So it happened that after a hasty luncheon I wound down the mountain to Parco, found Padre Stefano, explained my errand to him, found him intensely eager an sympathetic, and by five o'clock had him back at the convent with all that was necessary for the resting of the soul of the dead girl.

In the warm twilight, with the last light of the sunset pouring into the little cell through the window where almost a century ago Rosalia had for the last time said farewell to her lover, we gathered together to speed her tortured soul on its journey, so long delayed. Nothing was omitted; all the needful offices of the Church were said by Padre Stefano, while the light in the window died away, and the nickering names of the candles carried by two of the acolytes from San Francesco threw fitful flashes of pallid light into the dark recess where the white face had prayed to Heaven for a hundred years.

Finally, the Padre took the asperge from the hands of one of the acolytes, and with a sign of the cross in benediction while he chanted the _Asperges_, gently sprinkled the holy water on the upturned face. Instantly the whole vision crumbled to dust, the face was gone, and where once the candlelight had nickered on the perfect semblance of the girl dead so very long, it now fell only on the rough bricks which closed the window, bricks laid with frozen hearts by pitiless hands.

But our task was not done yet. It had been arranged that Padre Stefano should remain at the convent all night, and that as soon as midnight made it possible he should say the first mass for the repose of the girl's soul. We sat on the terrace talking over the strange events of the last crowded hours, and I noted with satisfaction that the Cavaliere no longer spoke of the Church with that hardness, which had hurt me so often. It is true that the Padre was with us nearly all the time; but not only was Valguanera courteous, he was almost sympathetic; and I wondered if it might not prove that more than one soul benefited by the untoward events of the day.

With the aid of the astonished and delighted servants, and no little help as well from Signora Valguanera, I fitted up the long cold Altar in the chapel, and by midnight we had the gloomy sanctuary beautiful with flowers and candles. It was a curiously solemn service, in the first hour of the new day, in the midst of blazing candles and the thick incense, the odor of the opening orange-blooms uniting up in the fresh morning air, and mingling with the incense smoke and the perfume of flowers within. Many prayers were said that night for the soul of the dead girl, and I think many afterwards; for after the benediction I remained for a little time in my place, and when I rose from my knees and went towards the chapel door, I saw a figure kneeling still, and, with a start, recognized the form of the Cavaliere. I smiled with quiet satisfaction and gratitude, and went away softly, content with the chain of events that now seemed finished.

The next day the alcove was again walled up, for the precious dust could not be gathered together for transportation to consecrated ground; so I went down to the little cemetery at Parco for a basket of earth, which we cast in over the ashes of

Sister Maddelena.

By and by, when Rendel and I went away, with great regret, Valguanero came down to Palermo with us; and the last act that we performed in Sicily was assisting him to order a tablet of marble, whereon was carved this simple inscription: —

HERE LIES THE BODY OF

ROSALIA DI CASTIGLIONI,

CALLED

SISTER MADDELENA.

HER SOUL

IS WITH HIM WHO GAVE IT.

To this I added in thought: —

"Let him that is without sin among you cast the first stone."

NOTRE DAME DES EAUX.

WEST of St. Pol de Leon, on the sea-cliffs of Finisterre, stands the ancient church of Notre Dame des Eaux. Five centuries of beating winds and sweeping rains have moulded its angles, and worn its carvings and sculpture down to the very semblance of the ragged cliffs themselves, until even the Breton fisherman, looking lovingly from his boat as he makes for the harbor of Morlaix, hardly can say where the crags end, and where the church begins. The teeth of the winds of the sea have devoured, bit by bit, the fine sculpture of the doorway and the thin cusps of the window tracery; gray moss creeps caressingly over the worn walls in ineffectual protection; gentle vines, turned crabbed by the harsh beating of the fierce winds, clutch the crumbling buttresses, climb up over the sinking roof, reach in even at the louvres of the belfry, holding the little sanctuary safe in desperate arms against the savage warfare of the sea and sky.

Many a time you may follow the rocky highway from St. Pol even around the last land of France, and so to Brest, yet never see sign of Notre Dame des Eaux; for it clings to a somewhat lower than the road, and between grows a stunted thicket of harsh and ragged trees, their skeleton white branches, tortured and contorted, thrusting sorrowfully out of the hard, dark foliage that still grows below, where the rise of land below the highway gives some protection. You must leave the wood by the two cottages of yellow stone, about twenty miles beyond St. Pol, and go down to the right, around the old stone quarry; then, bearing to the left by the little cliff path, you will, in a moment, see the pointed roof of the tower of Notre Dame, and, later, come down to the side porch among the crosses of the arid little grave-yard.

It is worth the walk, for though the church has outwardly little but its sad pic-turesqueness to repay the artist, within it is a dream and a delight. A Norman nave of round, red stone piers and arches, a delicate choir of the richest flamboyant, a High Altar of the time of Francis I., form only the mellow background and frame for carven tombs and dark old pictures, hanging lamps of iron and brass, and black, heavily carved choir-stalls of the Renaissance.

So has the little church lain unnoticed for many centuries; for the horrors and follies of the Revolution have never come near, and the hardy and faithful people of Finisterre have feared God and loved Our Lady too well to harm her church. For many years it was the church of the Comtes de Jarleuc; and these are their tombs that mellow year by year under the warm light of the painted windows, given long ago by Comte Robert de Jarleuc, when the heir of Poullaouen came safely to shore in the harbor of Morlaix, having escaped from the Isle of Wight, where he had lain captive after the awful defeat of the fleet of Charles of Valois at Sluys. And now the heir of Poullaouen lies in a carven tomb, forgetful of the world where he fought so nobly: the dynasty he fought to establish, only a memory; the family he made glori-ous, a name; the Chateau Poullaouen a single crag of riven masonry in the fields of

M. du Bois, mayor of Morlaix.

It was Julien, Comte de Bergerac, who rediscovered Notre Dame des Eaux, and by his picture of its dreamy interior in the Salon of '86 brought once more into notice this forgotten corner of the world. The next year a party of painters settled themselves near by, roughing it as best they could, and in the year following, Mme. de Bergerac and her daughter Héloïse came with Julien, and, buying the old farm of Pontivy, on the highway over Notre Dame, turned it into a summer house that almost made amends for their lost chateau on the Dordogne, stolen from them as virulent Royalists by the triumphant Republic in 1974.

Little by little a summer colony of painters gathered around Pontivy, and it was not until the spring of 1890 that the peace of the colony was broken. It was a sorrowful tragedy. Jean d'Yriex, the youngest and merriest devil of all the jolly crew, became suddenly moody and morose. At first this was attributed to his undisguised admiration for Mlle. Héloïse, and was looked on as one of the vagaries of boyish passion; but one day, while riding with M. de Bergerac, he suddenly seized the bridle of Julien's horse, wrenched it from his hand, and, turning his own horse's head towards the cliffs, lashed the terrified animals into a galop straight towards the brink. He was only thwarted in his mad object by Julien, who with a quick blow sent him headlong in the dry grass, and reined in the terrified animals hardly a yard from the cliffs. When this happened, and no word of explanation was granted, only a sullen silence that lasted for days, it became clear that poor Jean's brain was wrong in some way. Héloïse devoted herself to him with infinite patience,—though she felt no special affection for him, only pity, and while he was with her he seemed sane and quiet. But at night some strange mania took possession of him. If he had worked on his Prix de Rôme picture in the daytime, while Héloïse sat by him, reading aloud or singing a little, no matter how good the work, it would have vanished in the morning, and he would again begin, only to erase his labor during the night.

At last his growing insanity reached its climax; and one day in Notre Dame, when he had painted better than usual, he suddenly stopped, seized a palette knife, and slashed the great canvas in strips. Héloïse sprang forward to stop him, and in crazy fury he turned on her, striking at tier throat with the palette knife. The thin steel snapped, and the white throat showed only a scarlet scratch. Héloïse, without that ordinary terror that would crush most women, grasped the thin wrists of the madman, and, though he could easily have wrenched his hands away, d'Yriex sank on his knees in a passion of tears. He shut himself in his room at Pontivy, refusing to see any one, wanting for hours up and down, righting against growing madness. Soon Dr. Charpentier came from Paris, summoned by Mme. de Bergerac; and after one short, forced interview, left at once for Paris, taking M. d'Yriex with him.

A few days later came a letter for Mme. de Bergerac, in which Dr. Charpentier confessed that Jean had disappeared, that he had allowed him too much liberty, owing to his apparent calmness, and that when the train stopped at Le Mans he had slipped from him and utterly vanished.

During the summer, word came occasionally that no trace had been found of the unhappy man, and at last the Pontivy colony realized that the merry boy was dead. Had he lived he _must_ have been found, for the exertions of the police were perfect; yet not the slightest trace was discovered, and his lamentable death was acknowledged, not only by Mme. de Bergerac and Jean's family, — sorrowing for the death of their first-born, away in the warm hills of Lozère,- but by Dr. Charpentier as well.

So the summer passed, and the autumn came, and at last the cold rains of November — the skirmish line of the advancing army of winter — drove the colony back to Paris.

It was the last day at Pontivy, and Mlle. Héloïse had come down to Notre Dame for a last look at the beautiful shrine, a last prayer for the repose of the tortured soul of poor Jean d'Yriex. The rams had ceased for a time, and a warm stillness lay over the cliffs and on the creeping sea, swaying and lapping around the ragged shore. Héloïse knelt very long before the Altar of Our Lady of the Waters; and when she finally rose, could not bring herself to leave as yet that place of sorrowful beauty, all warm and golden with the last light of the declining sun. She watched the old verger, Pierre Polou, stumping softly around the darkening building, and spoke to him once, asking the hour; but he was very deaf, as well as nearly blind, and he did not answer.

So she sat in the corner of the aisle by the Altar of Our Lady of the Waters, watching the checkered light fade in the advancing shadows, dreaming sad day-dreams of the dead summer, until the day-dreams merged in night-dreams, and she fell asleep.

Then the last light of the early sunset died in the gleaming quarries of the west window; Pierre Polou stumbled uncertainly through the dusky shadow, locked the sagging doors of the mouldering south porch, and took his way among the leaning crosses up to the highway and his little cottage, a good mile away, — the nearest house to the lonely Church of Notre Dame des Eaux.

With the setting of the sun great clouds rose swiftly from the sea; the wind freshened, and the gaunt branches of the weather-worn trees in the churchyard lashed themselves beseechingly before the coming storm. The tide turned, and the waters at the foot of the rocks swept uneasily up the narrow beach and caught at the weary cliffs, their sobbing growing and deepening to a threatening, solemn roar. Whirls of dead leaves rose in the churchyard, and threw themselves against the blank windows. The winter and the night came down together.

Héloïse awoke, bewildered and wondering; in a moment she realized the situation, and without fear or uneasiness. There was nothing to dread in Notre Dame by night; the ghosts, if there were ghosts, would not trouble her, and the doors were securely locked. It was foolish of her to fall asleep, and her mother would be most uneasy at Pontivy if she realized before dawn that Héloïse had not returned. On the other hand, she was in the habit of wandering off to walk after dinner, often not coming home until late, so it was quite possible that she might return before Madame knew of her absence, for Polou came always to unlock the church for the low mass at six o'clock; so she arose from her cramped position in the aisle, and walked slowly up to the choir-rail, entered the chancel, and felt her way to one of the stalls, on the south side, where there were cushions and an easy back.

It was really very beautiful in Notre Dame by night; she had never suspected how strange and solemn the little church could be when the moon shone fitfully through the south windows, now bright and clear, now blotted out by sweeping clouds. The nave was barred with the long shadows of the heavy pillars, and when the moon came out she could see far down almost to the west end. How still it was! Only a soft low murmur without of the restless limbs of the trees, and of the creeping sea.

It was very soothing, almost like a song; and Héloïse felt sleep coming back to her as the clouds shut out the moon, and all the church grew black.

She was drifting off into the last delicious moment of vanishing consciousness, when she suddenly came fully awake, with a shock that made every nerve tingle. In the midst of the far faint sounds of the tempestuous night she had heard a footstep! Yet the church was utterly empty, she was sure. And again ! A footstep dragging and uncertain, stealthy and cautious, but an unmistakable step, away in the blackest shadow at the end of the church.

She sat up, frozen with the fear that comes at night and that is overwhelming, her hands clutching the coarse carving of the arms of the stall, staring' down into the dark.

Again the footstep, and again, slow, measured, one after another at intervals of perhaps half a minute, growing a little louder each time, a little nearer.

Would the darkness never be broken ? Would the cloud never pass? Minute after minute went like weary hours, and still the moon was hid, still the dead branches rattled clatteringly on the high windows. Unconsciously she moved, as under a magician's spell, down to the choir-rail, straining her eyes to pierce the thick night. And the step, it was very near! Ah, the moon at last! A white ray fell through the westernmost window, painting a bar of light on the floor of sagging stone. Then a second bar, then a third, and a fourth, and for a moment Héloïse could have cried out with relief, for nothing broke the lines of light, — no figure, no shadow. In another moment came a step, and from the shadow of the last column appeared in the pallid moonlight the figure of a man. The girl stared breathless, the moonlight falling on her as she stood rigid against the low parapet. Another step and another, and she saw before her—was it ghost or living man ? — a white mad face staring from matted hair and beard, a tall thin figure hall clothed in rags, limping as it stepped towards her with wounded feet. From the dead face stared mad eyes that gleamed like the eyes of a cat, fixed on hers with insane persistence, holding fascinating her as a cat fascinates a bird.

One more step, — it was close before her now! those awful, luminous eyes dilating and contracting in awful palpitations. And the moon was going out; the shadows swept one by one over the windows; she stared at the moonlit face for a last fascinated glance — Mother of God! it was — The shadow swept over them, and now only remained the blazing eyes and the dim outline of a form that crouched waveringly before her as a cat crouches, drawing its vibrating body together for the spring that blots out the life of the victim.

In another instant the mad thing would leap; but just as the quiver swept over the crouching body, Héloïse gathered all her strength into one action of desperate terror.

"Jean stop!"

The thing crouched before her paused, chattaring softly to itself; then it articulated dryly, and with all the trouble of a learning child, the one word, "_Chantes_!"

Without a thought, Héloïse sang; it was the first thing that she remembered, an old Provencal song that d'Yriex had always loved. While she sang, the poor mad creature lay huddled at her feet, separated from her only by the choir parapet, its dilating, contracting eyes never moving for an instant. As the song died away, came again that awful tremor, indicative of the coming death-spring, and again she sang, — this time the old Pange lingua,_ its sonorous Latin sounding in the deserted church like the voice of dead centuries.

And so she sang, on and on, hour after hour, — hymns and _chansons_, folk-songs and bits from comic operas, songs of the boulevards alternating with the _ Tantum ergo_ and the _O Filii et Felice._ It mattered little what she sang. At last it seemed to her that it mattered little whether she sang or no; for her brain whirled round and round like a dizzy maelstrom, her icy hands, griping the hard rail, alone supported her dying body. She could hear no sound of her song; her body was numb, her mouth parched, her lips cracked and bleeding; she felt the drops of blood fall from her chin. And still she sang, with the yellow palpitating eyes holding her as in a vice. If only she could continue until dawn! It must be dawn so soon! The windows were growing gray, the rain lashed outside, she could distinguish the features of the horror before her; but the night of death was growing with the coming day, blackness swept down upon her; she could sing no more, her tortured lips made one last effort to form the words, "Mother of God, save me!" and night and death came down like a crushing wave.

But her prayer was heard; the dawn had come, and Polou unlocked the porch-door for Father Augustin just in time to hear the last agonized cry. The maniac turned in the very act of leaping on his victim, and sprang for the two men, who stopped in dumb amazement. Poor old Pierre Polou went down at a blow; but Father Augustin was young and fearless, and he grappled the mad animal with all his strength and will. It would have gone ill even with him, — for no one can stand against the bestial fury of a man in whom reason is dead, — had not some sudden impulse seized the maniac, who pitched the priest aside with a single movement, and, leaping through the door, vanished forever.

Did he hurl himself from the cliffs in the cold wet morning, or was he doomed to wander, a wild beast, until, captured, he beat himself in vain against the walls of some asylum, an unknown pauper lunatic ? None ever knew.

The colony at Pontivy was blotted out by the dreary tragedy, and Notre Dame des Eaux sank once more into silence and solitude. Once a year Father Augustin said mass for the repose of the soul of Jean d'Yriex; but no other memory remained of the horror that blighted the lives of an innocent girl and of a gray-haired mother mourning for her dead boy in far Lozère.

THE DEAD VALLEY

I HAVE a friend, Olof Ehrensvärd, a Swede by birth, who yet, by reason of a strange and melancholy mischance of his early boyhood, has thrown his lot with that of the New World. It is a curious story of a headstrong boy and a proud and relentless family: the details do not matter here, but they are sufficient to weave a web of romance around the tall yellow-bearded man with the sad eyes and the voice that gives itself perfectly to plaintive little Swedish songs remembered out of childhood. In the winter evenings we play chess together, he and I, and after some close, fierce battle has been fought to a finish — usually with my own defeat — we fill our pipes again, and Ehrensvärd tells me stones of the far, half-remembered days in the fatherland, before he went to sea: stories that grow very strange and incredible as the night deepens and the fire falls together, but stones that, nevertheless, I fully believe.

One of them made a strong impression on me, so I set it down here, only regretting that I cannot reproduce the curiously perfect English and the delicate accent which to me increased the fascination of the tale. Yet, as best I can remember it, here it is.

"I never told you how Nils and I went over the hills to Hallsberg, and how we found the Dead Valley, did I ? Well, this is the way it happened. I must have been about twelve years old, and Nils Sjöberg, whose father's estate joined ours, was a few months younger. We were inseparable just at that time, and whatever we did, we did together.

"Once a week it was market day in Engel-holm, and Nils and I went always there to see the strange sights that the market gathered from all the surrounding country. One day we quite lost our hearts, for an old man from across the Elfborg had brought a little dog to sell, that seemed to us the most beautiful dog in all the world. He was a round, woolly puppy, so funny that Nils and I sat down on the ground and laughed at him, until he came and played with us in so jolly a way that we felt that there was only one really desirable thing in life, and that was the little dog of the old man from across the hills. But alas! we had not half money enough wherewith to buy him, so we were forced to beg the old man not to sell him before the next market day, promising that we would bring the money for him then. He gave us his word, and we ran home very fast and implored our mothers to give us money for the little dog.

"We got the money, but we could not wait for the next market day. Suppose the puppy should be sold ! The thought frightened us so that we begged and implored that we might be allowed to go over the hills to Hallsberg where the old man lived, and get the little dog ourselves, and at last they told us we might go. By starting early in the morning we should reach Hallsberg by three o'clock, and it was arranged that we should stay there that night with Nils's aunt, and, leaving by noon the next day, be home again by sunset.

"Soon after sunrise we were on our way, after having received minute instructions as to just what we should do in all possible and impossible circumstances, and finally a repeated injunction that we should start for home at the same hour the next day, so that we might get safely back before nightfall.

"For us, it was magnificent sport, and we started off with our rifles, full of the sense of our very great importance: yet the journey was simple enough, along a good road, across the big hills we knew so well, for Nils and I had shot over half the territory this side of the dividing ridge of the Elfborg. Back of Engelholm lay a long valley, from which rose the low mountains, and we had to cross this, and then follow the road along the side of the hills for three or four miles, before a narrow path branched off to the left, leading up through the pass.

"Nothing occurred of interest on the way over, and we reached Hallsberg in due season, found to our inexpressible joy that the little dog was not sold, secured him, and so went to the house of Nils's aunt to spend the night.

"Why we did not leave early on the following day, I can't quite remember; at all events, I know we stopped at a shooting range just outside of the town, where most attractive paste-foliage, serving so as beautiful marks. The result was that we did not get fairly started for home until afternoon, and as we found ourselves at last pushing up the side of the mountain with the sun dangerously near their summits, I think we were a little scared at the prospect of the examination and possible punishment that awaited us when we got home at midnight.

"Therefore we hurried as fast as possible up the mountain side, while the blue dusk closed in about us, and the light died in the purple sky. At first we had talked hilariously, and the little dog had leaped ahead of us with the utmost joy. Latterly, however, a curious oppression came on us; we did not speak or even whistle, while the dog fell behind, following us with hesitation in every muscle.

We had passed through the foothills and the low spurs of the mountains, and were almost at the top of the main range, when life seemed to go out of everything, leaving the world dead, so suddenly silent the forest became, so stagnant the air. Instinctively we halted to listen.

Perfect silence, — the crushing silence of deep forests at night; and more, for always, even in the most impenetrable fastnesses of the wooded mountains, is the multitudinous murmur of little lives, awakened by the darkness, exaggerated and intensified by the stillness of the air and the great dark: but here and now the silence seemed unbroken even by the turn of a leaf, the movement of a twig, the note of night bird or insect. I could hear the blood beat through my veins; and the crushing of the grass under our feet as we advanced with hesitating steps sounded like the falling of trees.

"And the air was stagnant, — dead. The atmosphere seemed to lie upon the body like the weight of sea on a diver who has ventured too far into its awful depths. What we usually call silence seems so only in relation to the din of ordinary experience. This was silence in the absolute, and it crushed the mind while it intensified the senses, bringing down the awful weight of inextinguishable fear.

"I know that Nils and I stared towards each other in abject terror, listening to our quick, heavy breathing, that sounded to our acute senses like the fitful rush of waters. And the poor little dog we were leading justified our terror. The black oppression seemed to crush him even as it did us. He lay close on it did us. He lay close on the ground, moaning feebly, and dragging himself painfully and slowly closer to Nils's feet. I think this exhibition of utter animal fear was the last touch, and must inevitably have blasted our reason — mine anyway; but just then, as we stood quaking on the bounds of madness, came a sound, so awful, so ghastly, so horrible, that it seemed to rouse us from the dead spell that was on us.

"In the depth of the silence came a cry, beginning as a low, sorrowful moan, rising to a tremulous shriek, culminating in a yell that seemed to tear the night in sunder and rend the world as by a cataclysm. So fearful was it that I could not believe it had actual existence: it passed previous experience, the powers of belief, and for a moment I thought it the result of my own animal terror, an hallucination born of tottering reason.

"A glance at Nils dispelled this thought in a flash. In the pale light of the high stars he was the embodiment of all possible human fear, quaking with an ague, his jaw fallen, his tongue out, his eyes protruding like those of a hanged man. Without a word we fled, the panic of fear giving us strength, and together, the little dog caught close in Nils's arms, we sped down the side of the cursed mountains, anywhere, goal was of no account: we had but one impulse — to get away from that place.

"So under the black trees and the far white stars that flashed through the still leaves overhead, we leaped down the mountain side, regardless of path or landmark, straight through the tangled underbrush, across mountain streams, through fens and copses, anywhere, so only that our course was downward.

"How long we ran thus, I have no idea, but by and by the forest fell behind, and we found ourselves among the foothills, and fell exhausted on the dry short grass, panting like tired dogs.

"It was lighter here in theopen, and presently we looked around to see where we were, and how we were to strike out in order to find the path that would lead us home. We looked in vain for a familiar sign. Behind us rose the great wall of black forest on the flank of the mountain: before us lay the undulating mounds of low foothills, unbroken by trees or rocks, and beyond, only the fall of black sky bright with multitudinous stars that turned its velvet depth to a luminous gray.

"As I remember, we did not speak to each other once: the terror was too heavy on us for that, but by and by we rose simultaneously and started out across the hills.

"Still the same silence, the same dead, motionless air — air that was at once sultry and chilling: a heavy heat struck through with an icy chill that felt almost like the burning of frozen steel. Still carrying the helpless dog, Nils pressed on through the hills, and I followed close behind. At last, in front of us, rose a slope of moor touching the white stars. We climbed it wearily, reached the top, and found ourselves gazing down into a great, smooth valley, filled half way to the brim with — what ?

"As far as the eye could see stretched a level plain of ashy white, faintly phosphorescent, a sea of velvet fog that lay like motionless water, or rather like a floor of alabaster, so dense did it appear, so seemingly capable of sustaining weight. If it were possible, I think that sea of dead white mist struck even greater terror into my soul than the heavy silence or the deadly cry — so ominous was it, so utterly unreal, so phantasmal, so impossible, as it lay there like a dead ocean under the steady stars. Yet through that mist _we must go_! there seemed no other way home, and, shattered with abject fear, mad with the one desire to get back, we started down the slope to where the sea of milky mist ceased, sharp and distinct around the stems of the rough grass.

"I put one foot into the ghostly fog. A chill as of death struck through me, stopping my heart, and I threw myself backward on the slope. At that instant came again the shriek, close, close, right in our ears, in ourselves, and far out across that damnable sea I saw the cold fog lift like a water-spout and toss itself high in writhing convolutions towards the sky. The stars began to grow dim as thick vapor swept across them, and in the growing dark I saw a great, watery moon lift itself slowly above the palpitating sea, vast and vague in the gathering mist.

"This was enough: we turned and fled along the margin of the white sea that throbbed now with fitful motion below us, rising, rising, slowly and steadily, driving us higher and higher up the side of the foothills.

"It was a race for life; that we knew. How we kept it up I cannot understand, but we did, and at last we saw the white sea fall behind us as we staggered up the end of the valley, and then down into a region that we knew, and so into the old path. The last thing I remember was hearing a strange voice, that of Nils, but horribly changed, stammer brokenly, The dog is dead ! and then the whole world turned around twice, slowly and resistlessly, and consciousness went out with a crash.

"It was some three weeks later, as I remember, that I awoke in my own room, and found my mother sitting beside the bed. I could not think very well at first, but as I slowly grew strong again, vague flashes of recollection began to come to me, and little by little the whole sequence of events of that awful night in the Dead Valley came back. All that I could gain from what was told me was that three weeks before I had been found in my own bed, raging sick, and that my illness grew fast into brain fever. I tried to speak of the dread things that had happened to me, but I saw at once that no one looked on them save as the hauntings of a dying frenzy, and so I closed my mouth and kept my own counsel.

"I must see Nils, however, and so I asked for him. My mother told me that he also had been ill with a strange fever, but that he was now quite well again. Presently they brought him in, and when we were alone I began to speak to him of the night on the mountain. I shall never forget the shock that struck me down on my pillow when the boy denied everything: denied having gone with me, ever having heard the cry, having seen the valley, or feeling the deadly chill of the ghostly fog. Nothing would shake his determined ignorance, and in spite of myself I was forced to admit that his denials came from no policy of concealment, but from blank oblivion.

"My weakened brain was in a turmoil. Was it all but the floating phantasm of delirium ? Or had the horror of the real thing blotted Nils's mind into blankness so far as the events of the night in the Dead Valley were concerned? The latter explanation seemed the only one, else how explain the sudden illness which in a night had struck us both down? I said nothing more, either to Nils or to my own people, but waited, with a growing determination that, once well again, I would find that valley if it really existed.

"It was some weeks before I was really well enough to go, but finally, late in September, I chose a bright, warm, still day, the last smile of the dying summer, and started early in the morning along the path that led to Hallsberg. I was sure I knew where the trail struck on to the right, down which we had come from the valley of dead water, for a great tree grew by the Hallsberg path at the point where, with a sense of salvation, we had found the home road. Presently I saw it to the right, a little distance ahead.

"I think the bright sunlight and the clear air had worked as a tonic to me, for by the time I came to the foot of the great pine, I had quite lost faith in the verity of the vision that haunted me, believing at last that it was indeed but the nightmare of madness. Nevertheless, I turned sharply to the right, at the base of the tree, into a narrow path that led through a dense thicket. As I did so I tripped over something. A swarm of flies sung into the air around me, and looking down I saw the matted fleece, with the poor little bones thrusting through, of the dog we had bought in Hallsberg.

"Then my courage went out with a puff, and I knew that it all was true, and that now I was frightened. Pride and the desire for adventure urged me on, however, and I pressed into the close thicket that barred my way. The path was hardly visible: merely the worn road of some small beasts, for, though it showed in the crisp grass, the bushes above grew thick and hardly penetrable. The land rose slowly, and rising grew clearer, until at last I came out on a great slope of hill, unbroken by trees or shrubs, very like my memory of that rise of land we had topped in order that we might find the dead valley and the icy fog. I looked at the sun; it was bright and clear, and all around insects were humming in the autumn air, and birds were darting to and fro. Surely there was no danger, not until nightfall at least; so I began to whistle, and with a rush mounted the last crest of brown hill.

"There lay the Dead Valley! A great oval basin, almost as smooth and regular as though made by man. On all sides the grass crept over the brink of the encircling hills, dusty green on the crests, then fading into ashy brown, and so to a deadly white, this last color forming a thin ring, running in a long line around the slope. And then? Nothing. Bare, brown,hard earth, glittering with grains of alkali, but otherwise dead and barren. Not a tuft of grass, not a stick of brushwood, not even a stone, but only the vast expanse of beaten clay.

"In the midst of the basin, perhaps a mile and a half away, the level expanse was broken by a great dead tree, rising leafless and gaunt into the air. Without a moment's hesitation I started down into the valley and made for this goal. Every particle of fear seemed to have left me, and even the valley itself did not look so very terrifying. At all events, I was driven by an overwhelming curiosity, and there seemed to be but one thing in the world to do, — to get to that Tree ! As I trudged along over the hard earth, I noticed that the multitudinous voices of birds and insects had died away. No bee or butterfly hovered through the air, no insects leaped or crept over the dull earth. The very air itself was stagnant.

"As I drew near the skeleton tree, I noticed the glint of sunlight on a kind of white mound around its roots, and I wondered curiously. It was not until I had come close that I saw its nature.

"All around the roots and barkless trunk was heaped a wilderness of little bones. Tiny skulls of rodents and of birds, thousands of them, rising about the dead tree and streaming on for several yards in all directions, until the dreadful pile ended in isolated skulls and scattered skeletons. Here and there a larger bone appeared, —the thigh of a sheep, the hoofs of a horse, and to one side, grinning slowly, a human skull.

"I stood quite still, staring with all my eyes, when suddenly the dense silence was broken by a faint, forlorn cry high over my head. I looked up and saw a great falcon turning and sailing downward just over the tree. In a moment more she fell motionless on the bleaching bones.

"Horror struck me, and I rushed for home, my brain whirling, a strange numbness growing in me. I ran steadily, on and on. At last I glanced up. Where was the rise of hill? I looked around wildly. Close before me was the dead tree with its pile of bones. I had circled it round and round, and the valley wall was still a mile and a half away.

"I stood dazed and frozen. The sun was sinking, red and dull, towards the line of hills. In the east the dark was growing fast. Was there still time? _Time_! It was not _that_ I wanted, it was _will !_ My feet seemed clogged as in a nightmare. I could hardly drag them over the barren earth. And then I felt the slow chill creeping through me. I looked down. Out of the earth a thin mist was rising, collecting in little pools that grew ever larger until they joined here and there, their currents swirling slowly like thin blue smoke. The western hills halved the copper sun. When it was dark I should hear that shriek again, and then I should die. I knew that, and with every remaining atom of will I staggered towards the red west through the writhing mist that crept clammily around my ankles, retarding my steps.

"And as I fought my way off from the Tree, the horror grew, until at last I thought I was going to die. The silence pursued me like dumb ghosts, the still air held my breath, the hellish fog caught at my feet like cold hands.

"But I won! though not a moment too soon.

As I crawled on my hands and knees up the brown slope, I heard, far away and high in the air, the cry that already had almost bereft me of reason. It was faint and vague, but unmistakable in its horrible intensity. I glanced behind. The fog was dense and pallid, heaving undulously up the brown slope. The sky was gold under the setting sun, but below was the ashy gray of death. I stood for a moment on the brink of this sea of hell, and then leaped down the slope. The sunset opened before me, the night closed behind, and as I crawled home weak and tired, darkness shut down on the Dead Valley."

POSTSCRIPT.

There seem to be certain well-defined roots existing in all countries, from which spring the current legends of the supernatural; and therefore for the germs of the stories in this book the Author claims no originality. These legends differ one from the other only in local color and in individual treatment. If the Author has succeeded in clothing one or two of these norms in some slightly new vesture, he is more than content.

Boston, July 3, 1895.

THE END.

The Codes Of Hammurabi And Moses
W. W. Davies

The discovery of the Hammurabi Code is one of the greatest achievements of archaeology, and is of paramount interest, not only to the student of the Bible, but also to all those interested in ancient history...

Religion ISBN: *1-59462-338-4*

QTY

Pages:132
MSRP $12.95

The Theory of Moral Sentiments
Adam Smith

This work from 1749. contains original theories of conscience amd moral judgment and it is the foundation for systemof morals.

Philosophy ISBN: *1-59462-777-0*

QTY

Pages:536
MSRP $19.95

Jessica's First Prayer
Hesba Stretton

In a screened and secluded corner of one of the many railway-bridges which span the streets of London there could be seen a few years ago, from five o'clock every morning until half past eight, a tidily set-out coffee-stall, consisting of a trestle and board, upon which stood two large tin cans, with a small fire of charcoal burning under each so as to keep the coffee boiling during the early hours of the morning when the work-people were thronging into the city on their way to their daily toil...

Childrens ISBN: *1-59462-373-2*

QTY

Pages:84
MSRP $9.95

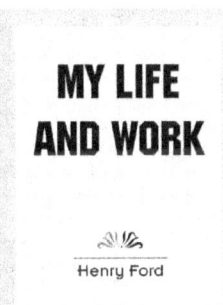

My Life and Work
Henry Ford

Henry Ford revolutionized the world with his implementation of mass production for the Model T automobile. Gain valuable business insight into his life and work with his own auto-biography... "We have only started on our development of our country we have not as yet, with all our talk of wonderful progress, done more than scratch the surface. The progress has been wonderful enough but..."

Biographies/ ISBN: *1-59462-198-5*

QTY

Pages:300
MSRP $21.95

The Art of Cross-Examination
Francis Wellman

QTY

I presume it is the experience of every author, after his first book is published upon an important subject, to be almost overwhelmed with a wealth of ideas and illustrations which could readily have been included in his book, and which to his own mind, at least, seem to make a second edition inevitable. Such certainly was the case with me; and when the first edition had reached its sixth impression in five months, I rejoiced to learn that it seemed to my publishers that the book had met with a sufficiently favorable reception to justify a second and considerably enlarged edition. ..

Reference   ISBN: *1-59462-647-2*

Pages:412

MSRP $19.95

On the Duty of Civil Disobedience
Henry David Thoreau

QTY

Thoreau wrote his famous essay, On the Duty of Civil Disobedience, as a protest against an unjust but popular war and the immoral but popular institution of slave-owning. He did more than write—he declined to pay his taxes, and was hauled off to gaol in consequence. Who can say how much this refusal of his hastened the end of the war and of slavery ?

Law   ISBN: *1-59462-747-9*

Pages:48

MSRP $7.45

Dream Psychology Psychoanalysis for Beginners
Sigmund Freud

QTY

Sigmund Freud, born Sigismund Schlomo Freud (May 6, 1856 - September 23, 1939), was a Jewish-Austrian neurologist and psychiatrist who co-founded the psychoanalytic school of psychology. Freud is best known for his theories of the unconscious mind, especially involving the mechanism of repression; his redefinition of sexual desire as mobile and directed towards a wide variety of objects; and his therapeutic techniques, especially his understanding of transference in the therapeutic relationship and the presumed value of dreams as sources of insight into unconscious desires.

Psychology   ISBN: *1-59462-905-6*

Pages:196

MSRP $15.45

The Miracle of Right Thought
Orison Swett Marden

QTY

Believe with all of your heart that you will do what you were made to do. When the mind has once formed the habit of holding cheerful, happy, prosperous pictures, it will not be easy to form the opposite habit. It does not matter how improbable or how far away this realization may see, or how dark the prospects may be, if we visualize them as best we can, as vividly as possible, hold tenaciously to them and vigorously struggle to attain them, they will gradually become actualized, realized in the life. But a desire, a longing without endeavor, a yearning abandoned or held indifferently will vanish without realization.

Pages:360

Self Help   ISBN: *1-59462-644-8*

MSRP $25.45

www.bookjungle.com *email: sales@bookjungle.com fax: 630-214-0564 mail: Book Jungle PO Box 2226 Champaign, IL 61825*

QTY

The Rosicrucian Cosmo-Conception Mystic Christianity by *Max Heindel*   ISBN: *1-59462-188-8* **$38.95**
The Rosicrucian Cosmo-conception is not dogmatic, neither does it appeal to any other authority than the reason of the student. It is: not controversial, but is: sent forth in the, hope that it may help to clear...   New Age/Religion Pages 646

Abandonment To Divine Providence by *Jean-Pierre de Caussade*   ISBN: *1-59462-228-0* **$25.95**
"The Rev. Jean Pierre de Caussade was one of the most remarkable spiritual writers of the Society of Jesus in France in the 18th Century. His death took place at Toulouse in 1751. His works have gone through many editions and have been republished...   Inspirational Religion Pages 400

Mental Chemistry by *Charles Haanel*   ISBN: *1-59462-192-6* **$23.95**
Mental Chemistry allows the change of material conditions by combining and appropriately utilizing the power of the mind. Much like applied chemistry creates something new and unique out of careful combinations of chemicals the mastery of mental chemistry...   New Age Pages 354

The Letters of Robert Browning and Elizabeth Barret Barrett 1845-1846 vol II   ISBN: *1-59462-193-4* **$35.95**
by *Robert Browning and Elizabeth Barrett*   Biographies Pages 596

Gleanings In Genesis (volume I) by *Arthur W. Pink*   ISBN: *1-59462-130-6* **$27.45**
Appropriately has Genesis been termed "the seed plot of the Bible" for in it we have, in germ form, almost all of the great doctrines which are afterwards fully developed in the books of Scripture which follow...   Religion/Inspirational Pages 420

The Master Key by *L. W. de Laurence*   ISBN: *1-59462-001-6* **$30.95**
In no branch of human knowledge has there been a more lively increase of the spirit of research during the past few years than in the study of Psychology, Concentration and Mental Discipline. The requests for authentic lessons in Thought Control, Mental Discipline and...   New Age/Business Pages 422

The Lesser Key Of Solomon Goetia by *L. W. de Laurence*   ISBN: *1-59462-092-X* **$9.95**
This translation of the first book of the "Lernegton" which is now for the first time made accessible to students of Talismanic Magic was done, after careful collation and edition, from numerous Ancient Manuscripts in Hebrew, Latin, and French...   New Age/Occult Pages 92

Rubaiyat Of Omar Khayyam by *Edward Fitzgerald*   ISBN: *1-59462-332-5* **$13.95**
Edward Fitzgerald, whom the world has already learned, in spite of his own efforts to remain within the shadow of anonymity, to look upon as one of the rarest poets of the century, was born at Bredfield, in Suffolk, on the 31st of March, 1809. He was the third son of John Purcell...   Music Pages 172

Ancient Law by *Henry Maine*   ISBN: *1-59462-128-4* **$29.95**
The chief object of the following pages is to indicate some of the earliest ideas of mankind, as they are reflected in Ancient Law, and to point out the relation of those ideas to modern thought.   Religion/History Pages 452

Far-Away Stories by *William J. Locke*   ISBN: *1-59462-129-2* **$19.45**
"Good wine needs no bush, but a collection of mixed vintages does. And this book is just such a collection. Some of the stories I do not want to remain buried for ever in the museum files of dead magazine-numbers an author's not unpardonable vanity..."   Fiction Pages 272

Life of David Crockett by *David Crockett*   ISBN: *1-59462-250-7* **$27.45**
"Colonel David Crockett was one of the most remarkable men of the times in which he lived. Born in humble life, but gifted with a strong will, an indomitable courage, and unremitting perseverance...   Biographies/New Age Pages 424

Lip-Reading by *Edward Nitchie*   ISBN: *1-59462-206-X* **$25.95**
Edward B. Nitchie, founder of the New York School for the Hard of Hearing, now the Nitchie School of Lip-Reading, Inc, wrote "LIP-READING Principles and Practice". The development and perfecting of this meritorious work on lip-reading was an undertaking...   How-to Pages 400

A Handbook of Suggestive Therapeutics, Applied Hypnotism, Psychic Science   ISBN: *1-59462-214-0* **$24.95**
by *Henry Munro*   Health/New Age/Health/Self-help Pages 376

A Doll's House: and Two Other Plays by *Henrik Ibsen*   ISBN: *1-59462-112-8* **$19.95**
Henrik Ibsen created this classic when in revolutionary 1848 Rome. Introducing some striking concepts in playwriting for the realist genre, this play has been studied the world over.   Fiction/Classics/Plays 308

The Light of Asia by *sir Edwin Arnold*   ISBN: *1-59462-204-3* **$13.95**
In this poetic masterpiece, Edwin Arnold describes the life and teachings of Buddha. The man who was to become known as Buddha to the world was born as Prince Gautama of India but he rejected the worldly riches and abandoned the reigns of power when...   Religion/History/Biographies Pages 170

The Complete Works of Guy de Maupassant by *Guy de Maupassant*   ISBN: *1-59462-157-8* **$16.95**
"For days and days, nights and nights, I had dreamed of that first kiss which was to consecrate our engagement, and I knew not on what spot I should put my lips..."   Fiction/Classics Pages 240

The Art of Cross-Examination by *Francis L. Wellman*   ISBN: *1-59462-309-0* **$26.95**
Written by a renowned trial lawyer, Wellman imparts his experience and uses case studies to explain how to use psychology to extract desired information through questioning.   How-to/Science/Reference Pages 408

Answered or Unanswered? by *Louisa Vaughan*   ISBN: *1-59462-248-5* **$10.95**
Miracles of Faith in China   Religion Pages 112

The Edinburgh Lectures on Mental Science (1909) by *Thomas*   ISBN: *1-59462-008-3* **$11.95**
This book contains the substance of a course of lectures recently given by the writer in the Queen Street Hail, Edinburgh. Its purpose is to indicate the Natural Principles governing the relation between Mental Action and Material Conditions...   New Age/Psychology Pages 148

Ayesha by *H. Rider Haggard*   ISBN: *1-59462-301-5* **$24.95**
Verily and indeed it is the unexpected that happens! Probably if there was one person upon the earth from whom the Editor of this, and of a certain previous history, did not expect to hear again...   Classics Pages 380

Ayala's Angel by *Anthony Trollope*   ISBN: *1-59462-352-X* **$29.95**
The two girls were both pretty, but Lucy who was twenty-one who supposed to be simple and comparatively unattractive, whereas Ayala was credited, as her Bombwhat romantic name might show, with poetic charm and a taste for romance. Ayala when her father died was nineteen...   Fiction Pages 484

The American Commonwealth by *James Bryce*   ISBN: *1-59462-286-8* **$34.45**
An interpretation of American democratic political theory. It examines political mechanics and society from the perspective of Scotsman James Bryce   Politics Pages 572

Stories of the Pilgrims by *Margaret P. Pumphrey*   ISBN: *1-59462-116-0* **$17.95**
This book explores pilgrims religious oppression in England as well as their escape to Holland and eventual crossing to America on the Mayflower, and their early days in New England...   History Pages 268

QTY

The Fasting Cure *by Sinclair Upton*
ISBN: *1-59462-222-1* **$13.95**

In the Cosmopolitan Magazine for May, 1910, and in the Contemporary Review (London) for April, 1910, I published an article dealing with my experiences in fasting. I have written a great many magazine articles, but never one which attracted so much attention... New Age/Self Help/Health Pages 164

Hebrew Astrology *by Sepharial*
ISBN: *1-59462-308-2* **$13.45**

In these days of advanced thinking it is a matter of common observation that we have left many of the old landmarks behind and that we are now pressing forward to greater heights and to a wider horizon than that which represented the mind-content of our progenitors... Astrology Pages 144

Thought Vibration or The Law of Attraction in the Thought World
ISBN: *1-59462-127-6* **$12.95**

by William Walker Atkinson Psychology/Religion Pages 144

Optimism *by Helen Keller*
ISBN: *1-59462-108-X* **$15.95**

Helen Keller was blind, deaf, and mute since 19 months old, yet famously learned how to overcome these handicaps, communicate with the world, and spread her lectures promoting optimism. An inspiring read for everyone... Biographies/Inspirational Pages 84

Sara Crewe *by Frances Burnett*
ISBN: *1-59462-360-0* **$9.45**

In the first place, Miss Minchin lived in London. Her home was a large, dull, tall one, in a large, dull square, where all the houses were alike, and all the sparrows were alike, and where all the door-knockers made the same heavy sound... Childrens/Classic Pages 88

The Autobiography of Benjamin Franklin *by Benjamin Franklin*
ISBN: *1-59462-135-7* **$24.95**

The Autobiography of Benjamin Franklin has probably been more extensively read than any other American historical work, and no other book of its kind has had such ups and downs of fortune. Franklin lived for many years in England, where he was agent... Biographies/History Pages 332

Name	
Email	
Telephone	
Address	
City, State ZIP	

☐ **Credit Card**   ☐ **Check / Money Order**

Credit Card Number	
Expiration Date	
Signature	

Please Mail to: *Book Jungle*
PO Box 2226
Champaign, IL 61825
or Fax to: *630-214-0564*

ORDERING INFORMATION

web*: www.bookjungle.com*
email*: sales@bookjungle.com*
fax*: 630-214-0564*
mail*: Book Jungle PO Box 2226 Champaign, IL 61825*
or PayPal *to sales@bookjungle.com*

Please contact us for bulk discounts

DIRECT-ORDER TERMS

**20% Discount if You Order
Two or More Books**
Free Domestic Shipping!
Accepted: Master Card, Visa,
Discover, American Express

www.ingramcontent.com/pod-product-compliance
Lightning Source LLC
Chambersburg PA
CBHW081158170626
46813CB00009B/3240